GirlChild

a novel

Morenike'

Written by Morenike'

Cover & Interior Design by David Provolo

For information, contact: authormorenike@gmail.com

First Edition

ISBN 13: 979-8-218-46249-9

Printed in the United States of America

Library of Congress Control Number: 2024913057

Morenike'

This book is dedicated to my dear uncle, Lee Matory;
thank you for all of your wisdom.

Chapter 1

Spring 1987
Huguenot Island, South Carolina

As the sun set over Huguenot Island, the ancestors of the Singleton family began to gather on the lowest sitting cloud over the Singleton house. Winter, the youngest ancestor, found a place to rest first. She was always anxious when dinner time in the Singleton household commenced. Winter died in 1968 in the Orangeburg Massacre. At the age of 21, she had not yet had the chance to enjoy a full life or raise a family of her own. When God summoned her and presented the opportunity to stay in limbo and watch over and guide Isata and Isaac, Winter jumped at the chance to live out a new purpose. Little did Winter know; she would sit on a council with other ancestors. Either God left out so many details in her assignment or she was so thrilled to stay behind that she had not paid much attention. There were so many rules to follow and unfortunately, she learned all of them the hard way.

"Moobe obuh gal-chile. Yuh uh is." Winter rolled her eyes and made space for Stepney Singleton. He was head ancestor and the council followed his every command. Stepney was the first and oldest ancestor chosen by God to guide the Singleton family. He died in 1739 during the Stono Slave Revolt and he never let a chance pass to remind Winter that he was in charge. Winter quickly learned that because Isaac was the head of household, the male ancestor always took lead. Stepney was head strong and had a direct line to God. Sibby was second in command to Stepney. She died in 1822 during the Denmark Vesey Slave Rebellion. Sibby also had a direct line to God but she believed in order and she and Stepney worked in perfect harmony. They trusted one another and had successfully guided Isaac and Isata since their union. Even when the council grew with Thunder, Moon, and Arrow when Isaac and Isata started having children, Stepney and Sibby still led with no issues. It was not until Winter joined them that they all began to squabble and second guess decisions.

Winter was a progressive thinker and very outspoken. She was also convincing when it came to swaying the other council members to see things her way when she disagreed with Stepney or Sibby. "Lawd hab mussy! Moobe gal-chile." Winter scoot over one last time to make room for Sibby. She knew that Stepney and Sibby sat at the head, but Winter always tried their patience. The rest of the ancestors finally joined them on the cloud. They watched as the Singleton children set the table. The oldest and only boy was Duck, then there was the second born, Sparrow, and the youngest, Little Dove. Ancestor Moon beamed with pride as she watched the children. When Isaac and Isata decided they wanted to start a family, Stepney and Sibby tasked Moon with naming the children. During Isata's pregnancies, Moon would spend time guiding her through walks in the woods and along the water. She would make sure Isata was greeted by birds and she would use the wind to whisper to Isata. Whenever Isata was asked by the children whey they were named after birds, she would simply respond, "We didn't want either of you to forget that the sky is the limit." Moon loved all of the children like they were her own; she considered Isata's pregnancies a joint effort and made it her duty to make sure her voice was heard anytime the council discussed parenting decisions.

Each ancestor, except Moon, had a favorite child whether they openly admitted it or not. Stepney and Arrow doted on Duck because he was so much like Isaac and they knew he would carry on the Singleton legacy like Isaac did. Thunder and Sibby liked Little Dove the most. She had the best qualities of both of her parents. Her spirit was pure and she kept the Singleton house from falling apart. Sparrow, on the other hand, was a problem child and no one advocated for her like Winter. Sparrow often challenged authority, did not hold her tongue, and openly denounced the Gullah way of life at every turn. The ancestors considered her to be destructive and lately, most of their meetings had been about something she had said or done. Winter came to her defense every time and saved her from the wrath of the ancestors on many occasions.

"I wonder what's for dinner tonight. Lord knows I miss food." Winter could feel her mouth water.

"Silly girl, it doesn't matter, you can't taste it." Arrow often had to remind Winter they were not of the world anymore.

"I know, Arrow, I'm just saying I miss good cooking is all."

They all looked on as Little Dove helped Isata carry dishes to the table. Moon couldn't help herself and applauded Little Dove. "Look, she helped Isata with the perloo tonight. She's just growing up so fast."

Sibby nodded in agreement, "she helped with the cornbread too. Watch what I tell ya, Little Dove is gone be a good wife one day."

Winter chimed in, "Sparrow made a sweet potato pie for dessert." As usual, everyone ignored her; some of the ancestors were still getting over Sparrow's latest lashing out.

Sparrow was a senior in high school and was set to graduate in two weeks. The plan was to work in the family restaurant for a year before she left to go off to college. She wanted to be a lawyer and was in the top of her class at a special academy on the mainland. A month ago, she demanded that she no longer be addressed by any of her family in their Gullah language or called by her nickname. She took the stance that the Creole would prevent her from being successful in the future but was too prideful to admit that non-Gullah speakers at school had been bullying her. Isaac and Isata argued every night for a week along with the ancestors that watched from above. Winter was able to convince everyone it was a phase and that Sparrow would learn to appreciate their culture in her own time. Stepney fed this excuse to Isaac when he prayed for guidance. Isaac was able to convince Isata that Sparrow would come around and it was time to stop treating her like a baby.

Isaac rubbed his hands together in satisfaction as he watched his wife and youngest daughter set dishes down on the table. Isata removed the lids off the pots before sitting down. "Everything looks delicious as always; you girls are showing ya Mama up in the kitchen." Little Dove beamed with pride as she clasped hands with her mother and sister. They all bowed their heads in prayer. Isaac began to say grace, "gee we food wa we need dus day yah an eby day…" Sparrow cleared her throat and interrupted him. Isaac opened his eyes and lifted his head to see that Sparrow was staring him down. He finished, "thank you Father. Amen." Isata began fixing Isaac's plate. "So your father can't say grace in Gullah either?" Sparrow ignored her mother and asked Duck to pass the cornbread so she could cut it. She was not in the mood to argue tonight. "Thank you for respecting my wishes, Daddy. One day, when I'm a successful lawyer, it will all make sense." She served slices of cornbread to her father then her brother before placing slices on her mother and sister's plate.

They ate in silence. Isata was visibly annoyed with Sparrow and Isaac was too busy enjoying dinner to notice. Duck and Little Dove learned early on to stay out of anything between their sister and parents. After dinner, Little Dover wrapped up the leftovers for Isaac and Duck to take across the way to their grandmother, Mama Maggie. All of Isaac's siblings still lived on the island and they usually ate dinner together but Isaac and Isata were off from the family restaurant tonight. Mama Maggie wasn't feeling well earlier and wasn't able to join them for dinner. But Little Dove and Sparrow insisted Mama Maggie test taste what they cooked. They were always trying to one up each other in the kitchen; in a friendly competition of sorts. Mama Maggie was their teacher and judge. Duck called out as he and Isaac walked out the door, "we be back!"

The girls helped Isata clean the kitchen until it was spotless. "I'm gonna have another slice of pie on the porch, ya'll care to join me?" Isata began slicing the pie and placed it on a napkin. Little Dove opted for more. As Isata fixed another slice, Little Dove broke out into a coughing fit. While Isata tended to her, Sparrow removed a strainer from the cabinet and hid it behind her back. She knew it was going to be another one of those long nights when Little Dove broke out into a coughing fit. "No pie for me Mama, I'll be in my room." Isata was too busy trying to calm Little Dove down to notice Sparrow grab the broom on her way out the kitchen. Stepney and Sibby looked at one another with concern as they watched Sparrow tip toe to her room with the strainer and broom. Stepney dismissed everyone but Winter. "Watch her. Sibby and I have some where to be. Don't leave your watch until Sparrow is asleep. We don't need any trouble tonight. Understood?" Winter sighed, "yea, I got it." She knew when Sparrow snuck out the kitchen she would be in for another long night.

Duck and Isaac were back from Mama Maggie's and Duck's room was right across from the room she shared with Little Dove. Sparrow closed her bedroom door as not to draw attention to herself. She didn't want Duck to catch her with the broom and strainer or he would pick on her and call her crazy. Sparrow plopped down on her bed and laid the broom on the floor. She placed the strainer on her makeshift nightstand. She sighed as she surveyed the modest room she and Little Dove shared. "I can't wait to leave this place and experience civilization. Why can't we just live normal lives?" Sparrow often spoke aloud to herself, venting her frustrations in the open. Winter watched Sparrow from above, doing the same. "She is so misunderstood. She just wants to experience life outside this island." Moon suddenly appeared and sat down next to Winter. "So, you're on Sparrow duty tonight? I can watch her if you have something to do."

Winter sighed out of frustration. "No, I can watch her but I resent the fact that Stepney and Sibby look at her as a problem. Sparrow is special."

"Believe me, this I know. I was with Isata during every pregnancy. All them children something special. Little Dove be everyone's favorite, but Sparrow gone save this family one day."

Winter glanced at Sparrow to make sure she was okay before turning her full attention to Moon. "What do you mean by that, save us from what?"

Moon's kind eyes smiled at Winter. "Now you know me can't tell you that."

Winter gently corrected Moon. "You have to say 'I,' not 'me.' Stepney said we have to speak properly now, remember."

Moon rolled her eyes at Sparrow below. "I forgot about that silly girl's new rule. But you know what I mean; we aren't allowed to share prophecies from God."

"Do Stepney and Sibby know?"

"Of course not; God give it to me when I watched over Isata. I can't say what it is, I can only provide guidance when it is time."

"Wow. That's big Moon. I can't remember the last time Stepney or Sibby had a prophecy. I'm still waiting on one."

"It will happen when God thinks you're ready."

"I can't tell; I feel like He doesn't trust me. It's not like I can summon Him and I know Stepney doesn't vouch for me."

"Nonsense; if God didn't trust you, you wouldn't be here. And don't mind Stepney, he's always been the way he is."

"You're right, I shouldn't let doubt creep in. I need to be strong for Sparrow. I always feel like she's going to need me, especially lately."

Moon stood up and gathered her things. "It's just growing pains. You have to stop living through Sparrow; it's her life, not yours. I'm headed back, don't stay out too long."

"I won't; goodnight Moon."

When Little Dove entered their bedroom, Sparrow was sitting in the middle of the floor counting money from a mason jar. It had become Sparrow's nightly ritual lately and Little Dove always joined her although the amount only changed by a few dollars every other day. The Singleton children spent their evenings after school and their summers working at their family restaurant, Singleton's Kitchen. They were paid in home-cooked meals and tips. Sparrow had been saving her tips for the past year in preparation for college. The plan was to take introductory courses at a community college before heading north to a university of her choosing. "One thousand, two hundred and forty-five dollars and sixty-five cents and counting. If only Mama and Daddy would let me work more shifts instead of making me stay home with Mama Maggie." She started stuffing the money back into the mason jar. Little Dove gathered all the loose change. "You will have enough before school. Don't worry about it. You can even take some of my shifts, I don't mind staying with Mama Maggie." Sparrow kissed her sister on the forehead. "And that's why I love you so much. I see you had another coughing fit earlier, how are you feeling?"

"I'll be fine; you don't have to worry about me. Mama and Te Ola think I have asthma. Can you believe Te Ola suggested Mama take me to a doctor on the mainland? Te Ola the most talented medicine woman I know and she say go to the doctor."

"You and I both know you don't have no asthma. When you gone tell them the truth?"

Little Dove put her hand up to silence Sparrow. "What truth is that? Ain't nobody ever seen the hag but you and no offense sis but everybody think you do and say things out of spite these days. What I ever done wrong for a hag to be leeching on me?"

Sparrow turned down her sheets and climbed into her twin bed. "I don't know what you ever done. All I know is what I feel and see. I'm not crazy and I'm not making it up to spite the family."

Little Dove climbed into her bed and fluffed her pillow before turning off the lamp on the nightstand between their beds. "It's asthma, Sparrow. Don't make it into a big deal. Goodnight."

Sparrow rolled over with her back to her sister. "Goodnight Dovey."

Sparrow waited until she could hear a light snore from the other side of the room. Little Dove was finally asleep. Sparrow got out of bed and grabbed the broom and strainer. She placed the broom in the corner by Little Dove's bed and she quietly hung the strainer off the doorknob. She admired her handy work. "Not tonight, bitch." All she could do now was wait. She grabbed a flashlight and book and returned to bed to read. Winter yawned as she watched on. "Why can't you just go to bed, Sparrow?" Winter decided she wouldn't mention Sparrow's mischief to the other ancestors; she was not in the mood to hear Stepney's mouth.

For the past two years, Sparrow claimed that a hag had been creeping into her bedroom at night and feeding on Little Dove. It wasn't an entirely crazy notion. Everyone knew hags existed; the issue was that no one could see or feel this particular hag but Sparrow. The ancestors couldn't even see the accused and when Sparrow prayed for guidance, the ancestors turned the other cheek. Sibby chalked it up to being another form of lashing out on Sparrow's part. Stepney even suggested that no hag would leech on a sweet spirit like Little Dove when Sparrow was the one who needed to be punished. Winter felt bad for Sparrow and although she couldn't see the hag either, she didn't disregard Sparrow's prayers. One night, while on watch, Winter answered Sparrow's call for help and guided her to confide in Mama Maggie. Winter soon regretted that decision when Mama Maggie told Sparrow not to interfere with 'God's plan.' Winter never told anyone about her interference and Sparrow never confided in another adult about the hag again.

Chapter 2

Sparrow awoke in panic at the sound of her book falling onto the floor. She didn't realize she had fallen asleep. She looked over to see that Little Dove was still asleep. Sparrow readjusted in bed to get more comfortable. She pulled a saltshaker from under her pillow and placed it on her nightstand. It was almost midnight and she needed to be alert and prepared. She still hadn't figured out how, but the hag was coming in through a crevice somewhere in the house. There was no doubt in her mind the hag would make an appearance tonight. The only time Little Dove had a coughing fit or felt lightheaded was when the boo hag was near. Everyone knew Little Dove was a relatively healthy child. Te Ola did everything to prevent illness in any of the children. She always said, "the future is in all of you; the Singleton way of life cannot prevail without our babies."

Winter grew irritable as she watched from above. All the ancestors had turned in for the night. The moment she saw Sparrow reach for the saltshaker she knew she should have gone to Stepney. Winter felt a weird ache in the pit of her stomach. "What are you up to silly girl?" She began pacing back and forth in worry. If Sparrow caused a scene tonight, Winter wouldn't hear the end of it if she didn't warn Stepney and Sibby. She weighed her options. She wanted to please God so that he would trust her with a prophecy one day; but pleasing God meant being obedient to Stepney. "I'm sorry Sparrow, not tonight." Winter turned to go track down Stepney when the smell hit her. It wafted across her nostrils sending her into an instant spiral of panic. The smell, potent and disgusting, reminded her of rotten eggs and carcass. Winter fell to her knees and called out for Sparrow as if Sparrow could hear her directly.

The sound of the wind banging against the shutters made Sparrow jump. She gagged at the smell of her room. She climbed out of bed as quick as she could but it was too late. She could feel the tears forming in her eyes; sadness set upon her as the temperature in her room dropped. It was freezing. She went to grab the saltshaker when a low voice stopped her dead in her tracks. "Are you looking for this?" It was too late. Sparrow turned around to see that the boo hag was on top of Little Dove's chest. The saltshaker lay above Little Dove's head.

Sparrow tried to scream but the words would not escape her mouth; they were stuck in her throat. The boo hag was rid of skin with pulsing, blue veins. Her body was red and bloodied. Her eyes were a piercing gray. Little Dove was rendered helpless as the hag pinned her down. Little Dove's body occasionally ticked, evidence of life. "You must know by now girl; you cannot defeat me. Your sweet sister's energy keeps me strong." The hag taunted Sparrow; her wails sounded like that of a banshee.

Winter couldn't believe her eyes. No one had ever seen the boo hag before; everyone thought Sparrow was lying. Winter could feel the fear coursing through Sparrow's veins. She could feel the hollowness that Little Dove was stuck in like a nightmare. Her mind went into overdrive as she asked herself, "*Who was this boo hag? Why could she see it now? What did It want with Little Dove? Why didn't the strainer or broom work?*" Winter jumped to her feet; she hated to leave the girls behind but she had to get the rest of the ancestors.

Sparrow felt frozen in place. It took all her strength to take a step closer to her sister's bed as she watched the hag feast. She tried screaming but her voice remained trapped. The hag paused to taunt her. "Are you going to stop me? Of course not, you're not strong enough." Sparrow closed her eyes and allowed anger and frustration to overtake her, providing her with the strength to charge toward the hag. She yelled as she jumped on the bed. "Leave my sister alone!" She fought with all her might as the hag flew around the bed, still engaged in stealing Little Dove's essence. Sparrow covered her sister's face with a pillow to break the connection.

Isaac and Isata entered the girl's bedroom just as the ancestors returned to the cloud. All Isata could see was Sparrow smothering Little Dove as Little Dove's body seized. Isata mustered all of her strength to throw Sparrow to the floor. But Isaac saw more, he felt more as he ran to Sparrow's side. He looked into her bewildered eyes and shook his head in understanding. It was a warm, spring night and their room was freezing; he could smell the remnants of a rotting carcass floating across the room. Duck ran across the hall and Isaac ordered him to fetch Ola. Isata held Little Dove as she awoke in a coughing fit. Through her tears, Isata screamed at Sparrow, "what the hell is wrong with you? You could have killed her." Isaac could see the rage in Sparrow's eyes. He grabbed her before she was able to lunge for her mother. He threw her over his shoulder as she kicked and screamed, "I saved her, you never believed me before, but tonight I saved her!"

The ancestors watched in awe as Isaac carried Sparrow out of the house across the way to Mama Maggie's. Winter had gathered them just in time for them to see the hag before it disappeared. All was quiet until Stepney roared, "Why did you wait so late to alert us?" He began shouting orders, "Moon, watch over Isata and Little Dove. Arrow and Thunder, you must guard Maggie's while Sparrow is there. Sibby, find out who that hag is and where it came from!" Winter stood there confused and powerless. How could he be upset with her when she did what she was supposed to do? Stepney turned to Winter, his face hard and scary, "You. Tell me everything you saw."

Sparrow sat on the edge of her grandmother's bed in tears. She was still in shock. How could Isata think she would try to harm Little Dove? Mama Maggie spoke as if she could hear Sparrow thinking aloud. "Leave it be. You need rest. You just battled a hag." Sparrow laid across the bed but she knew sleep would not come to her; she was too afraid to sleep. Mama Maggie filled a sock with frankincense and placed it against Sparrow's forehead. The aroma filled Sparrow's nostrils. Mama Maggie placed the sock under a pillow and commanded her granddaughter to sleep. "Rest. Tomorrow will come and it will be a better day." Sparrow placed her head across the pillow as she was told. All she could remember was her grandmother's prayers before she fell into a deep sleep.

Chapter 3

The next morning, Sparrow rolled over to see the other side of the bed was empty. She could hear hushed voices coming from the kitchen. The smell of oysters and grits filled the room. "They been in there talking about you." Sparrow wiped the sleep out of her eyes to see Duck sitting in Mama Maggie's rocking chair. She sat up in bed and offered as much of a smile she could muster. "Is that so? Everybody thinks I'm crazy now." Duck handed Sparrow a bowl of oysters and grits with a biscuit. She thanked him by diving headfirst into the food. Last night had taken a lot of her energy. She savored every bite. "I don't think you're crazy. Daddy told me what he smelled and felt in that room. Te Ola confirmed it. Mama was just scared is all; all she could see was you smothering Dovey."

Sparrow sopped up the bowl with the biscuit and licked her fingers. She handed the bowl back to her brother and downed a glass of water on the nightstand. "How's Dovey?" Duck stood up and looked out the window as his uncles and cousins prepared to head to their rice field. "She's mostly been in and out of sleep. Too weak to leave the bed right now and Mama is being dramatic and won't let her get up. The hag must have really done a job on her." Sparrow's heart skipped a beat. Little Dove had never been bed ridden after the hag rode her; Sparrow felt like a failure. "What did I do wrong, Duck? I tried to stop it." Te Ola entered the room and interrupted, "You did nothing wrong. Duck, give us a minute. Take them dishes back to the kitchen." Duck did as he was told and closed the door behind him. Ola sat on the edge of the bed next to Sparrow and held her hand. Before Ola could speak, there was a light tap at the door followed by Isata yelling, "Don't you go back there!" then Little Dove's gentle voice, "it will be fine, Mama. It's only Sparrow. She won't hurt me."

Little Dove opened the bedroom door slowly and kindly asked Ola to leave the room with her gentle eyes. When she and Sparrow were alone, she climbed into the bed next to her sister and grabbed Sparrow's hand. "Thank you for saving me. I finally felt it; saw what you were seeing. I know you're not crazy, sister." Sparrow rolled her eyes and got out of the bed. She got up and looked out the window to see Duck joining their father to head to the rice field. "Try telling Mama that; she hate me." Little Dove got up and joined Sparrow, hugging her from behind. "The only thing you need to worry about is leaving this place. Ain't no hags at college I suppose. Mama about to be so clingy that I'll probably be stuck here. You can work all my shifts to make extra money to get out of here. I'm sure gone miss you but I want you to be happy." Sparrow turned around and embraced her baby sister. A sole tear ran down her check. She would miss Little Dove but not even their sisterly bond could heal the part of Sparrow that desperately wanted to escape her family and the island. "I'll miss you too, Dovey. I love you."

Sparrow returned home from her grandmother's a few days later on her 18th birthday. Isaac was adamant about them celebrating as a family over dirty cake for breakfast like they did every year. Sparrow was hesitant but agreed to come home. Isata had finally calmed down and allowed Little Dove to move around freely. They gathered at the table and Duck took lead by slicing the cake for everyone. The tension in the room was obvious. For some reason, despite Isaac and Ola confirming that a hag attacked Little Dove, Isata was still upset with Sparrow. For the past few days, Sparrow and Isata avoided one another like the plague and Sparrow spent her days at Mama Maggie's place.

They sat and ate in silence. Sparrow played in her cake; she didn't have an appetite and she simply wasn't in the mood to be around her mother. She pushed her chair back from the table and rose. "Can I go to my room?" Isaac responded with a nod; he didn't feel like starting an argument. Sparrow walked to her room and closed the door. She laid across her bed and buried her head in her pillow. The tears came naturally. She had no clue why she was so upset. It was her birthday; she should be on her second slice of dirty cake by now and laughing with her family. Instead she was miserable, and her mother wasn't speaking to her.

The ancestors watched from above. No one spoke immediately. Sparrow wasn't an angel to say the least but finally seeing the hag made some of the ancestors draw back their reservations about the troublesome child. Moon was the first to speak up. "Now is the time for forgiveness and comfort. We must guide Isata to go to Sparrow and embrace her." Winter spoke next, "I agree. Isata must also apologize." Stepney was quiet; he put his finger up to let them know he needed a moment. Stepney then turned to Moon and instructed her to do what needed to be done. They were right; Isata needed to embrace Sparrow and apologize. All of the ancestors had seen the hag and everyone knew Sparrow would never do anything to harm Little Dove.

After breakfast, Duck and Little Dove cleaned the kitchen. Isaac left for the restaurant. Isata sat on the porch to clear her mind. It was the perfect time for the ancestors to come to her. Isata spoke to herself, "why am I so angry with that child? Me know she meant no harm but she could have killed my baby. Lord help me." Isata's call summoned Moon. The wind picked up and swirled around Isata's chair. Moon whispered to Isata, "Humble yourself." Isata closed her eyes and took heed. The wind stopped and Moon left Isata.

Isata went back into the house and went to the girls' room. She knocked on the door gently and entered before there was a response. Little Dove was comforting a crying Sparrow. Isata asked Little Dove to give her some time alone with Sparrow. Little Dove kissed Sparrow on the forehead before leaving the room. Isata sat on Little Dove's bed and faced Sparrow.

"Why are you crying my love?"

Sparrow shrugged. "I don't know. I'm just overwhelmed today."

"It's your birthday, we should be celebrating."

"Does it feel like a celebration to you? You've been avoiding me, Mama. You act like you hate me."

Isata got up and embraced a reluctant Sparrow. "No, no, look at me. I could never hate you. I admit the last few days have been weird but as a mother this has been hard for me; watching you grow up and change the way you have. You hate the Gullah way of life and I was adjusting to that. Then suddenly you say you see a hag and I find you smothering your sister. Please tell me you can see how this would be hard for me too."

Sparrow pulled back from Isata. "It's hard for me too! You think I want to see hags and listen to spirits? I want to live a normal life. I want off this island. I hate it here."

"This all you've ever known; life has been good to you. How could you hate our way of life?"

"You'll never understand. I don't expect you to; just know when I leave here, it'll take a miracle for me to come back."

Later that night, Sparrow waited until there wasn't a peep in the house. She grabbed her suitcase and mason jar of money and tip toed out of the front door. She made her way in the dark to the bridge where she met her cousin, August. August had borrowed one of the pickup trucks the family used in the rice field. The plan was to drop Sparrow off at the bus station on the mainland. August and Sparrow were close like sisters and although August loved the Gullah way, she understood Sparrow's yearning to experience a normal life. A life where people didn't judge her and her family by their Creole and way of life; a world where change and technology was embraced. Sparrow wanted a forward looking life.

August finally pulled the old pickup truck into the bus station parking lot. She leaned over and hugged Sparrow tight. She couldn't believe this was finally happening. "I must really love you cousin because if the family find out I dropped you off, it'll be my hide and you know it."

"No one will know, you sneak out all the time."

"Mhmm. You just be sure to write me as soon as you get somewhere safe."

"Of course I will; I won't forget that you did this for me."

"You better not. I love you."

"I love you too."

Sparrow got out of the truck and walked into the bus station. Moon and Winter watched from above. Winter was concerned, "what do we do? Should we go get Stepney?" Moon smirked as she watched Sparrow brave on. "No, you silly girl, it's her destiny. Leave her be. She'll be back."

Chapter 4

Summer 1997
New York City, New York

Sparrow rolled over and turned off the alarm clock on her nightstand. The sun began to peek through the blinds. It was almost time for her mother to call from the restaurant like she did every other morning. Sparrow rolled back over and smiled as she watched her boyfriend, David, sleep peacefully without a care in the world. She began to plant soft kisses on his face and arms. He groaned to let her know that he was awake. He reached for her waist and pulled her closer.

"We have some time."

She chuckled. "No, we don't. Mama's gonna call any second."

"Damn that woman and these early morning calls."

"Hey, watch it, that's my Mama you're talking about."

He spooned her and nibbled on her ear. He began to playfully beg. "Please."

Sparrow hiked up her night gown and pulled off her panties. The phone rang just as she was about to give in to him. David groaned in frustration and rolled his eyes as she hopped out of bed and ran to the kitchen to answer the phone.

"Hey Mama."

"How did you know it was me?"

Sparrow sighed. "It's always you, Mama. You're the reason I ever got a house phone."

"Oh hush. How are you?"

Sparrow rolled her eyes, glad that her mother couldn't see her. "I'm fine; just like I was when you called the day before yesterday. We really should make these weekly calls."

Isata sucked her teeth. "There's too much island gossip for weekly phone calls. You wouldn't dare not answer my calls."

"Of course not Mama. So tell me what's new."

"Just the usual. The restaurant is doing really well and Duck has been selling rice like crazy. He's been doing so well since Little Dove is supposed to be on bed rest. You should really come home and visit, don't you miss my cooking?"

It never failed; every time they talked Isata tried her best to convince Sparrow to come home to visit. It had been ten years since they had seen one another, and these phone calls had become the glue to their relationship.

"Of course, I miss your cooking. And what do you mean, supposed to be on bed rest? Is she sick?"

Isata caught herself and tried to clean it up. "Walking pneumonia, she'll be fine."

"I hope she feels better. But now isn't a good time with work and all. David is on track to make partner at the firm."

"There's always an excuse. Sparrow, you can't go without family forever. We need you as much as you'll need us one day."

"I hear you, Mama. I said it isn't a good time right now."

Sparrow changed the subject so not to upset Isata any further. The last thing she wanted to do was argue. After they finished gossiping, Isata passed the phone to Isaac then Little Dove. They were all up early prepping for the breakfast shift at Singleton's Kitchen.

They talked until it was time for Sparrow to get ready for work. She ended her call and returned to the bedroom to tend to David before preparing for her day.

Life on the island had changed drastically since Sparrow's departure. South Carolina had become a hot spot for resorts and tourism. Singleton's Kitchen was a tour stop which sent the family into overdrive. The restaurant had always been a hit amongst locals but tourism had taken them over the edge. They were now open seven days a week and even sold rice from their field wholesale to local resorts. The only problem they had the were encroaching land developers that always approached Mama Maggie and neighboring families about their land. Mama Maggie refused to sell but some of the other locals were considering cashing in on a big payday while others were losing their land and homes due to heirs' property. It wouldn't be long before the island was commercial property. But besides the greedy land developers, life couldn't be better for the Singleton family.

Isata made the executive decision not to relay this news to Sparrow whenever they talked. She wasn't even sure if it would bring Sparrow home. Isaac often suggested they ask Sparrow for legal advice about the situation but even Mama Maggie agreed that it wasn't a good idea to reveal what was happening on the island. Mama Maggie often reiterated that Sparrow's decision to come home needed to be one of her own choosing; manipulating her would only make her rebel. The family decided to trust Isata and Mama Maggie but their patience was tested every time an attorney was at Mama Maggie's doorstep. It was like they were preying on her because they would only approach her when she was alone and the rest of the family was at work or at the restaurant.

Mama Maggie reassured them all that she could handle herself and that even in her old age, she was still cognizant of what was going on around her. She made it known that she wouldn't sign any paperwork; over her dead body would she lose the family land. She intended to pass it on to her children and grandchildren and nothing would step in the way of that. Mama Maggie consulted with the ancestors often but never revealed to anyone else that she knew Sparrow would be their saving grace one day. She often had dreams in which the ancestors would come to her and show her the future of her family. The Singleton Way would live on, no matter what.

Chapter 5

Little Dove stood on her tip toes and tried to get a bag of rice off the top of a shelf. Isaac came to the rescue and stopped her. "You know you not supposed to put your arms above your head like that; you'll choke that baby." Little Dove stood back and let her father retrieve the bag of rice. She rubbed her eight-month-old belly and whispered an apology to the baby. Isaac continued to scold her. "You shouldn't be here anyway. I thought August was working all your shifts from now on. Ola says you should be on bedrest." Little Dove ignored him and turned her attention to her mother. "Do you think we should have told Sparrow about the baby?"

"I think we should wait honey, don't you?"

"I guess. I don't know. I think it will make her want to come home."

Isata kissed Little Dove on the forehead. "Let's wait until the baby gets here, ok?"

Little Dove sighed in disappointment, "Ok Mama."

Little Dove's pregnancy was a sensitive subject. Sparrow didn't know her little sister was with child. Over the past five years, Little Dove and her husband, Gentry, had suffered six miscarriages and one stillbirth. Each pregnancy almost brought Sparrow home to visit and each loss proved to be a disappointment. Sparrow's theory was that the hag had made her sister barren but Isata wouldn't stand to hear it and Little Dove's faith wouldn't let her give up.

This pregnancy felt different to Little Dove. Even Gentry said the way the baby kicked and moved around gave him hope. Little Dove wanted to share the news with her sister badly but everyone agreed it was best to wait in case of another heartbreak. Even Ola suggested modern medicine which was a surprise to them all. It was evident everyone was on the same page; this baby must survive.

Later that night, the Singleton women gathered for prayer at Mama Maggie's. It had become a ritual of theirs every time Little Dove was with child. They prayed over her and called on the ancestors to protect her and the baby. Tonight, all the aunts were present: Esther, Ola, and Lillie. They believed there was strength in numbers.

They sat in a circle on the living room floor, barefoot with their legs crossed. Little Dove sat in the middle of the circle with her eyes closed. Isata began the prayer and then they each took turns offering words. At Little Dove's turn, she called out a special prayer for Sparrow's return home. The aunts called out in agreement. By the end of the night, Little Dove was confident that her baby was safe and that Sparrow would be home soon.

Isata and Ola helped Little Dove up from the floor. Isata dusted off Little Dove's dress before planting a kiss on her forehead. Little Dove decided to ask what everyone would have been thinking.

"When are we going to tell Sparrow about the land?"

Ola chimed in quickly, "I think we need to focus on one thing at a time. Let's think about the baby right now."

Little Dove retorted. "We can't ignore the elephant in the room. My baby needs a future and that includes the land. Sparrow should know. She's a lawyer, she can help."

Lille rubbed Little Dove's back to comfort her; "now, now child, don't go getting yourself worked up over things that are out of our control. God will work it all out. Let's listen to Ola; the baby is the priority here."

Isata was conflicted but she showed solidarity with Ola. "I agree, we worry about the baby first. When it is time, Sparrow will know all there is to know about the land, ok my love?"

Little Dove turned her back to her mother and aunts. She folded her arms in frustration. "Whatever you say. Baby first."

The ancestors had been watching on as the Singleton women called out in prayer for the baby and as they disagreed about discussing the land with Sparrow. They, too, wanted this baby to survive. They, too, wanted to save the land. Little Dove had been through so much over the years experiencing miscarriage after miscarriage. Somehow, Little Dove and Gentry managed to stay strong. After prayer, the ancestors broke rank and Sibby, Moon, and Winter stayed behind. They typically watched the women fellowship over food until they dispersed. Winter had so many questions. She became more and more anxious as Little Dove neared her due date. She turned to Sibby and Moon, "Is there nothing we can do to ensure this baby lives?" Moon only offered, "We should not interfere with God's work." Sibby added, "but I think all the signs are there, this baby shall live." Winter stopped pacing and sat down. "What if we can get Sparrow to come home?" Moon spoke up before Sibby could answer. "We haven't guided Sparrow since she ran away. She has not sought out our help either. She denounced the

Gullah way." Winter didn't seem to care about that, "she's still family, Moon. Right Sibby?"

Sibby agreed, "Moon is right. No one can make that stubborn child do anything. She will come home when she is ready. Do not appear to her unless she seeks out our help. Am I understood?" Winter's silence satisfied Sibby.

After all these years, Winter still advocated for Sparrow. She was convinced Sparrow would be the saving grace of the family. Sparrow was in the dark about Little Dove's pregnancy and she had no idea about the severity of resort developers wanting the family land. Winter didn't know how but some way she would get Sparrow to come home whether the other ancestors agreed with her or not. She was willing to take the risk. It was almost time for the ancestral council meeting. Stepney, Arrow, and Thunder would be returning soon. The Singleton women had decided to take a walk along the water. The council meeting began with Stepney giving his usual speech. He was mostly talking to Winter about walking a straight path and doing God's work by serving the family. Winter was tired of being treated like a child. Sibby spoke on their concerns for Little Dove and her pregnancy; even the male ancestors were worried. Sibby did a good job of reassuring them everything would be fine. Meanwhile, the Singleton women walked barefoot along the water. They talked about how well the restaurant and rice field was doing. They talked of Little Dove and Gentry's future with the baby. All was well until Little Dove doubled over in pain. She cried out to the sky. It was early but it was time; the baby was coming. Ola instructed some of the women to go get towels and a bucket of hot water. "This baby coming now. Ain't no better place to birth it than here in nature."

Isata tore a piece of her skirt and wiped Little Dove's forehead. She held her daughter's hand as she wailed in pain. "Baby girl, look at me, you can do this."

"It's too soon, Mama, and Gentry's not here!"

"This is God's timing. We don't question that."

Little Dove responded with a scream as Ola checked her cervix. Her body began to shake in a violent fit, conjuring up a storm. It began to thunder, and lightning struck as Little Dove contracted. The other women returned with a sweetgrass basket, a bucket of hot water, and towels. They circled Ola, Isata, and Little Dove in a chant of prayer. Ola yelled at Little Dove, "Trust your body baby, you can do this." Tears run down Little Dove's face as her body jerked; it was time to push. She had done this before; it should have come naturally but she felt no control over her body, just pain. She called out to the ancestors for help but there was only lightning and thunder and then it began to sprinkle rain.

Ola counted off and instructed Little Dove to push. It took all her might but Little Dove pushed until she was told to stop. Isata talked her through breathing until it was time to push again. Ola yelled out, "She's crowning already, give me one more big push!" Little Dove did as she was told and pushed through the worse pain of her life. "It's a girl!" Ola held the baby and pat it on the back but there was no response. Ola cleaned the baby off with a towel. She tried CPR a few times. She finally hung her head in disappointment. Isata began to cry. The aunts kept praying. Ola wrapped the baby in a towel and handed the baby to Little Dove. She sat up in tears. How could this have happened again? She pat the baby on the back praying for a cry in return but there was no answer. Little Dove placed the baby in the sweetgrass basket and mustered up the strength to get up and carry the basket out to the water. "This is my offering, Lord. Please don't let it be in vain."

The ancestors had dismissed their meeting and only Moon and Winter had been left behind to witness the birth. Winter was frantic, "We have to do something. This baby has to live." Moon was in shock. She thought Sibby had been so reassuring because she knew something the rest of them didn't. "What can we do? It's too late, Winter." Winter paced back and forth. "No it's not. I can fix this. I can help. It's my purpose." Winter took a step off the cloud and disappeared before Moon could respond. Moon looked bewildered; what just happened?

The Singleton women stood in solidarity and held hands, chanting a prayer as the water carried the basket. A strike of lightning hit the basket and Winter entered the baby's body. A wave crashed down and carried the basket back to shore. Little Dove broke the prayer circle and ran to the basket as she swore she heard cries. The baby was alive. Isata fell to her knees and lifted her hands in praise. "Sparrow is coming home."

Chapter 6

Sparrow tossed and turned as a storm raged on outside. David lay sound asleep on the other side of the bed. Sparrow woke in a panic and heard a voice whisper to her, *it is time, come home.* The phone rang and Sparrow hopped out of bed to catch it before David woke up.

"Hello?"

"Sparrow!"

"Daddy, is that you? It's almost midnight; is everything okay?"

"I'm sorry to call so late but this news couldn't wait."

"What news? Tell me what's going on."

"Mama just called me at the restaurant. I'm still here cleaning up. Little Dove just had a baby girl. She's alive and healthy. Can you believe it?"

Sparrow was tongue tied. "Wait a minute; Little Dove was pregnant, and no one told me?"

"We didn't want you to worry, you know, in case the baby didn't survive. She was eight months along, but the baby is fine."

"I can't believe this; it's a miracle! Is Little Dove okay?"

"She's fine, just wore out is all. Ola delivered the baby and it wasn't breathing at first. Almost sent them into a panic but they prayed, and God answered."

"I really can't believe it, wow."

"Your mama wants to know when you're coming home."

Without hesitation, Sparrow proclaimed, "I'll be on the first bus I can. I just need to work out some things at the office first."

"Well, we'll see you soon Auntie Sparrow."

Sparrow's smile could be heard through the phone. "I like the sound of that."

Moon sat with her head held low as the ancestors chewed her out. They had been yelling at her all night. *How could you let her do this? Why weren't you watching her? Did you help Winter plan this?* Even Sibby was upset, and it was hard to make her mad. Moon didn't know what to say or do to defend herself. She was still in shock at Winter's actions. Stepney roared causing thunder to lash across the sky. "I will fix this!" Moon knew that meant Stepney and Sibby would have to consult with God and that a sacrifice must be made; she just hoped it didn't mean taking this baby from Little Dove.

Isaac came home from the restaurant with good news. Sparrow was coming home. It was the best news the Singleton family had gotten in a while. Isata insisted that Little Dove, Gentry, and the baby stay with her and Isaac for a little while. They would stay in Duck's old room. Isaac went straight to Little Dove when he walked in the house. She was surrounded by Isata, Gentry, and Ola. He wanted to see his granddaughter.

"Ya'll move back and let me see this pretty baby."

Little Dove handed the baby over to Isaac. "Here Daddy, you can hold her."

"She's beautiful. You did a fine job." He noticed a patch of gray hair in the baby's head. "Oh she been here before. What's her name?"

"Well, seeing as God gave me a healthy baby girl, I named her GirlChild."

"I see. Well, GirlChild, I'm your Paw."

Two days later, Sparrow took a nineteen-hour bus ride back home to South Carolina. Isaac was going to meet her at the bus station in Charleston. The ride gave her flashbacks of the night she ran away. She thought about how excited and scared she had been; much like the way she was feeling now. She couldn't believe her family kept such a secret from her for the past eight months. The bus finally pulled into the station and Sparrow was at the door before the bus could even stop. She could see her father waiting at the platform. She hurried off and grabbed her bags before running toward Isaac. "Daddy!" She dropped her bags at her feet and embraced her father. Tears rolled down her face as she inhaled his scent and took in his warm smile. She couldn't believe it had been ten years.

Isaac picked up her bags and headed to the truck. Sparrow followed him and jumped into the driver's seat. "I wanna drive, see if I remember where I'm going." Isaac obliged and tossed her the keys before getting into the passenger's seat. "I can't imagine you do much driving in New York with the subway and all."

"David and I share a car, but we mostly take the subway or a taxi. It's easier."

"Why didn't he come? We been dying to meet him."

"He couldn't get off work in time." Sparrow was in no rush to tell her family she was with a white man. She could hear them now; "H*ow come you bring this buckra here!"*

It took them about an hour and half to get to the restaurant from the bus station, but Sparrow wanted to see Isata before she went to the house. The dirt parking lot was full of cars. and two tour buses. There was a line out the door. Isaac instructed Sparrow to park in the back so they could go in through the kitchen. As soon as Sparrow stepped foot in the kitchen, she was bombarded by some of her uncles and cousins that were cooking and plating dishes. She gave out hugs and kisses. Isata and some of the aunts were in the dining area taking orders and serving. Sparrow watched her mother from the serving window. Isata was still as beautiful as ever; with cinnamon colored skin and piercing brown eyes. As soon as Isata spotted Sparrow, she dropped what she was doing and ran to the kitchen.

They embraced one another in tears.

"My baby girl, it's been such a long time. Oh my God, you look just like Mama Maggie."

"Thank you Mama. You need help with anything?"

"I'm so glad you asked. Get an apron and help us in the dining room."

Sparrow hesitated for a moment. "Uhh, is the menu the same?"

"With a few changes here and there; you'll catch on quick."

For the next couple of hours, Sparrow helped her family like she did in the old days. She even saw some familiar faces and made a good number of tips. But all the ripping and running finally caught up with her and wore her out. She couldn't believe she used to do this almost every day as a child. It felt weird being back home.

Sparrow worked through the extended lunch hour until everyone was served and the restaurant was cleared out. She was exhausted and ready to go lay down. Isaac handed the keys to Isata to take Sparrow home. He would be staying behind for the evening crowd.

As Isata drove home, she couldn't help but to sneak glances at Sparrow and squeeze her daughter's hand. Sparrow looked out the window in awe at how much everything had changed. There were paved roads and traffic lights. There were convenience and retail stores. There was major construction taking place for a resort. She never thought she would see the day that Huguenot Island took a step forward into the future. Sparrow caught Isata looking at her and turned her attention to her mother.

"What is it?"

"Nothing baby, I'm just so glad to have you home. I haven't laid eyes on you in forever. It's been ten years."

"I know, Mama. I'm sorry for that. I should have come home sooner."

"Little Dove is gone be so happy to see you."

"I'm excited to see my baby sister; what did she name the baby?"

"Aht aht, I won't be spilling the beans; Little Dove will tell you. She is a special little something though, the way she come in this world."

"I can't wait to hold her and smell her. They say babies have the best smell."

"You thinking about having one soon? With that David?"

Sparrow chuckled at her mother's snarkiness. "It's in the cards for us, I'm sure, just not now. We both are so focused on our careers."

"Why didn't he come anyway? Don't he wanna meet your family? We wanna meet him, for certain. We need to know this man you plan on spending your life with."

"Save that for the next trip, Mama. He couldn't get away from work at the last minute. He is on track to be partner. He can't drop everything he's doing."

"I understand. Just make sure he gets down here one day."

"I will. I promise."

Isata changed the subject. "How long you staying?"

"I'll be here two weeks then I gotta get back to work. I don't want my workload to get too crazy."

"Two weeks, huh? Ain't seen ya in ten years and two weeks is all you can spare for family?"

Sparrow could sense her mother's frustration. "Mama, please, let's be peaceful. I promise I'll come back down when I have more time."

"You're right. I'm sorry. I'm just so overwhelmed with emotion. I can't believe my baby is home."

They finally pulled into the dirt cul de sac they called Singleton Way. It consisted of six homes, all occupied by the Singleton family. The cul de sac originally had three houses until Isaac and his brothers built the other three a little after Sparrow was born. The original homes were smaller two and three bedroom homes. The newer homes were three and four bedroom homes with wrap around porches. Some of the family resided on Singleton Way and the rest lived in a neighborhood on the mainland close to the restaurant. The Singleton's were a hard laboring family and very proud of their way of life.

Isata pulled into their driveway and honked the horn twice. They were greeted by Little Dove's husband, Gentry. He embraced Sparrow and grabbed her bags. Before he could get out a word, Sparrow yelled, "where's Little Dove?" and shot into the house. Sparrow ran room to room until she laid her eyes on Little Dove. Ola was sitting the corner in a rocking chair with the baby while Little Dove slept. Sparrow entered the room quietly and instantly teared up. Ola got up to hug her and handed the baby over to Sparrow with no question. Sparrow couldn't believe her eyes. She was holding a miniature Little Dove. The baby was wide awake and cooed. She was only 3 days old and alert. Ola gently nudged Little Dove to wake her and welcome her sister. Little Dove had been exhausted and experiencing some difficulties since delivery, but she remained her calm self. Little Dove sat up in bed and extended her arms for Sparrow to come to her.

"Sparrow! Oh how I've missed you big sister. Come here!"

Sparrow handed the baby back to Ola and slowly sat down on the bed to lay in her sister's arms. "My sweet Little Dove. Can you believe I'm here? How are you feeling?"

"I'm tired but I'm so happy you're here."

The baby began to fuss so Ola handed her to Little Dove who placed the baby to her breast to feed. "Meet your niece, GirlChild."

"GirlChild? You are so Gullah, I swear."

Little Dove laughed and then winced in pain. "It's what God wanted."

"Are you okay? What's wrong?"

"Just a little chest pain. Childbirth takes a toll on the body. I'll be fine in no time."

"Are you sure? Have you been to see a doctor yet?"

Little Dove broke out into a coughing fit. Ola handed her a cup of water. "Why would I do that when we have the best medicine woman right here?"

Ola checked Little Dove's forehead with the palm of her hand. "Just wanna make sure you not running a fever. Give me that baby, I'll give her a bottle while you talk to your sister. And Sparrow, I'll pretend you didn't just insult your dear old aunt."

Sparrow apologized. "I didn't mean anything by it." She waited until Ola left the room with the baby to continue. "Maybe you should consider seeing someone for a checkup; isn't that customary after having a baby?"

Little Dove shook her head and waved off Sparrow's suggestion. "Nonsense. I'll be fine. I need to ask you something."

"Anything; I feel like we have so much to catch up on."

"First things first, now that you are home, I can officially ask you."

"Ask me what?"

"Will you be GirlChild's god mother? It is my only wish; Gentry's too."

Sparrow was shocked but honored "That's a huge responsibility but I swear to you and Gentry, I will guard her with my life. But she needs a nickname; I can't call her GirlChild."

Little Dove thought about how much her sister had and hadn't changed all at the same time. Sparrow was still ashamed of the Gullah way of life. "No nicknames. Promise me. You'll love her like your own."

"I promise, Little Dove, but let's talk about something else; this subject just seems so finite."

"You and your lawyer words. I'm not trying to scare you. I just wanted it to be known that you are her godmother." Little Dove prayed the title she bestowed upon her sister meant she would come home more often. She knew how much the family needed Sparrow although the elders wouldn't admit it.

"You got it; anything you need."

"Perfect; we're going to a pediatrician on the mainland tomorrow. I want you to join us."

"I'll be there sis."

Sparrow and Little Dove spent the new few hours talking, laughing, and crying. It was like they had never left one another's side. Little Dove had another coughing fit and Sparrow suggested she get some rest while Sparrow go see Mama Maggie. As Sparrow closed the bedroom door behind her, she couldn't help but wonder, *is that hag still riding my sister?*

Chapter 7

Sparrow walked across the street to her grandmother's house. She just knew Mama Maggie would chew her out for taking so long to come back to South Carolina. Every time they talked on the phone, Mama Maggie cursed New York for taking her grand baby away from her family. Sparrow knocked on the door and it flew open. Mama Maggie had been anxiously waiting on her and snatched her into her arms. They hugged for what seemed like forever. There was no need for words, it was understood that their undying love for one another was still present. Sparrow followed Mama Maggie into the living room, and they sat across from one another.

"My dear Sparrow, you look so good."

"Mama says I look like you."

Mama Maggie slapped her knee. "Don't I know it!"

They both broke out into a girlish giggle.

Mama Maggie asked about her trip into town. "Was the ride smooth? Did you stop by the restaurant?"

"Yes and yes. I got a chance to see everyone. I can't believe I'm actually here after all these years. Can you?"

"I can. I knew you would be back. The ancestors told me. God told me."

Sparrow rolled her eyes. "Mama Maggie, really? If it weren't for the baby, who knows when I would have come back."

"The ancestors have never failed me. It was only a matter of time. Just like the birth of that fine baby Little Dove done had; it was only a matter of time."

"I can't believe she's really here. Little Dove asked me to be her godmother."

"I hope you ready for that responsibility."

"I believe so. I'm going to do my best."

"How long you staying?"

"Two weeks; then I gotta get back to work."

"Two weeks? Well, that just won't do. We need more time."

"You sound like Mama; more time for what?"

Mama Maggie's brow furrowed. "I take it no one has told you about what's going on around here?"

"What do you mean?"

Mama Maggie paused before she spoke. She wondered if it was too soon to tell Sparrow about the attorney some land developers sent to speak to some of the islanders about selling their land for another resort. Sparrow had just gotten home and she didn't want to scare her away but Mama Maggie knew it was the work of God bringing Sparrow back home at a time when the family needed her most. She decided to put it off and let Sparrow get acclimated to being back home first.

"Oh it's nothing child; just old lady talk. We'll talk about it later. Let's get some tea brewing while you tell me all about that man you been shacking up with."

Sparrow threw her head back and laughed. "Mama Maggie! Times have changed. I'm a modern woman doing modern things."

"Modern my tail! Don't make no sense to let a man have his cake and eat it too. Why he ain't come down with you? Don't he wanna know where and who you come from?"

"Like I told Mama, David is busy with work. I promise one day, we both will make the trip down so ya'll can meet him."

"I hope it happens before I die."

"Mama Maggie! Don't say that!"

"Oh chile we all gotta get up outta here one day. You best believe that; that's why you gotta love on us while we here."

Sparrow and Mama Maggie spent the rest of the afternoon gossiping and catching up. A few of the aunts and cousins stopped by to see Sparrow. It was like a family reunion. Sparrow felt warm and happy being surrounded by true love. It was a feeling she hadn't felt in a while. In South Carolina, she had community. In New York, it was just her and David.

They were so focused on work that they didn't have time to build community. She could count on one hand how many friends she had and they were all people she had met at work. She didn't even have hobbies. She expressed all of this to Mama Maggie begrudgingly; she didn't want her grandmother to think she had become a failure. Mama Maggie assured her that she had so much more life to live and that she hadn't even begun to fulfill her purpose yet. Mama Maggie proclaimed, "there's still time. Your story just begun." They talked until evening when Isata sent Duck to retrieve Sparrow. Isata needed help prepping family dinner. Sparrow told her grandmother goodbye for now and promised to come back the next day after the baby's doctor appointment.

Sparrow was so excited to see Duck. They stood outside for a few minutes catching up before Isata summoned her to the kitchen. "Get in here and help me with this food." Sparrow went into the house and went to work right away. It was like she had never left home; she and Isata worked in sync to cook a meal and dessert that would be ready as soon as Isaac got off work and stepped in the door. By the time they were finished, the dining room table had a spread like no other.

It looked like a holiday meal. There was shrimp, crab, oyster stew, red rice, collard greens, okra soup, yams, and peach cobbler.

Isaac walked into the house just as Duck finished helping Sparrow set the table. Isaac went to wash up. Isata called out to Gentry and Little Dove. The baby was asleep and would stay in her bassinet. Gentry helped Little Dove out of bed and held her arm as he helped her walk into the dining room and take a seat at the table. Once everyone was seated, they held hands and Isaac said prayer. Isata fixed the men's plates first and then Sparrow fixed a plate for herself and Little Dove.

Isaac beamed with pride as he watched his family fellowship. His family felt complete again. He didn't realize until that very moment how much Sparrow had been missed. Sparrow caught Isaac looking at her and her gaze met his; they smiled at one another, a silent agreement that it was good she was home. Isaac complimented the chefs, "You two put your foot off in this meal. These collards taste like heaven."

Sparrow took responsibility for her work. "That's my doing; I'm glad I haven't lost my touch. I haven't cooked them in so long."

Duck chimed in. "You and David eat out a lot?"

"We do, unfortunately; with the hours we work, I don't have time to cook. Chinese food is my best friend."

Isata couldn't believe her ears. "I've never had Chinese food a day in my life. No wonder you don't have a ring yet; you need to cook that man a proper Gullah meal."

Little Dove stepped in to save her sister. "Oh Mama stop it; we all know Sparrow is a big shot lawyer up there in the big city. She's busy."

Sparrow didn't want to argue so she changed the subject. "I brought something for dinner. I'll be right back."

She got up from the table and went into her old bedroom where Gentry had put her bags. She rifled through her suitcase and pulled out a bottle of Dom Perignon. She headed into the kitchen and grabbed as many glasses as she could carry and returned to the dining room.

"I think this calls for a celebratory toast."

Gentry asked, "What's the occasion?"

"I'm home, Gentry! And you're a father! What isn't there to celebrate?"

She began pouring glasses of champagne but skipped Little Dove. "None for you baby sis. You're breast feeding."

Little Dove understood. "It's fine, maybe next time."

Once everyone else had a glass, Sparrow sat back down, and they raised their glasses to toast. Sparrow gave a short speech.

"To family. My family. One that I have taken for granted and missed so much. To my strong, little sister and Gentry. I admire your strength and determination in starting a family of you own. I love you all. This toast is for Girlchild and the future of this family."

Everyone clinked glasses and shouted in agreement. "To GirlChild, to family!"

The ancestors watched from above as the Singleton family, finally reunited, fellowshipped with one another. Although it was a joyous occasion, because Sparrow was finally home, there was major tension amongst the ancestors. They could not ignore the elephant amongst them. Winter was gone. Sibby and Stepney had been gone for the past two days and had finally returned. Stepney called a council meeting. Moon was nervous for what was to come as she knew Sibby and Stepney had been consulting with God about what to do next. Thunder and Arrow had been silent on the matter. They both knew there was nothing they could say to justify Winter's actions or calm Stepney down.

Stepney had been pacing. He finally bellowed down on a cloud and called the council meeting to order. The other ancestors turned their attention to him.

"I think we all know why we're here tonight. One of us has betrayed this council and disobeyed God. For that, a remedy must be made."

Before he could continue, Moon interrupted. "I just want it to be known, none of us knew this would happen. There was no way to stop her."

Stepney softened his tone before he spoke to Moon. "I have come to terms with that; it was beyond your control. You have served this council gallantly and it was my mistake and anger that led me to think otherwise."

Moon nodded her head in thanks. She was relieved that Stepney could see the bigger picture now.

Sibby stepped up to add. "We blame none of you. Winter's actions were solely her own, but I fear we must all make a sacrifice for her choices."

Silence filled the space between them. They were all thinking the same thing. Would God call Winter back to her rightful place? Would that mean the death of GirlChild; the baby they had all prayed for, for so long?

Arrow boldly asked. "Does the baby get to live?"

Thunder added, "We can all agree that Little Dove has suffered enough; it would not be fair to let her have time with the baby and then take her away."

Stepney stepped in and shut everyone down. "These decisions are not ours to make. We are only here to guide the family and protect them. God will deliver the verdict in due time, and we will be there to do what we must. That is all."

Stepney had put his foot down. It was clear he wasn't open to any more questions or concerns about the matter. He ended the meeting and dismissed them all. When there was no one left but he and Sibby, he expressed himself to Sibby. "What have we agreed to Sibby? What have we done to this family?" Sibby didn't know what to say but offered, "Only God knows."

After dinner, Sparrow helped Isata with the dishes while the men folk sat on the porch and finished off the champagne. It had been such a good day for them all. Isata hummed a tune while she dried the wet dishes Sparrow passed over. Sparrow felt so safe being back home. She felt love swallowing her whole and for once, she didn't want to let it go. When they were done in the kitchen, they joined the men on the porch. Little Dove had returned to the room to tend to the baby.

As time wound down, Duck said his goodbyes so he could take Mama Maggie a plate before he went home. He was scheduled to open the restaurant with his uncles the next morning. Sparrow hugged her big brother as tight as she could before he left. Isaac and Isata decided to go get ready for bed, leaving Gentry and Sparrow behind. Sparrow hadn't talked to her brother in law in a while, but they caught up like they never missed a beat. Gentry was an honorable man, and she was grateful to God for placing him in Little Dove's life. They had never met in person, but they talked on the phone whenever Little Dove called.

Gentry and Little Dove had met in undergrad at the University of South Carolina just like Isaac and Isata had many years ago. Gentry was an engineering major and Little Dove was a business management major. When Gentry told the story of how they met, he tried to humbly avoid the fact that their courtship was the reason Little Dove didn't finish her program. By the third date, they knew they were destined to be together, and he vowed to love, protect, and provide. They got married at the courthouse after Gentry finished school and Little Dove returned to help manage Singleton's Kitchen.

Unlike Gentry and Little Dove, Isata and Isaac had a wedding. After a house fire killed her parents, Isata went to the live with an aunt and uncle in the mountains. When she went off to the University of South Carolina, she met Isaac. They got married after they both graduated. Isata's uncle wanted to honor his brother, Isata's late father, so he made sure he paid for an extravagant wedding and gave her away. Because of their wedding, Isaac and Isata wished Little Dove would have allowed them to do the same for her. But Little Dove was a simple girl, she didn't require much, and Gentry's love was enough.

Sparrow expressed her thanks to Gentry for agreeing to let her be the baby's godmother.

"Little Dove told me you both wanted me to be the baby's godmother. You don't know how much that means to me."

"Anything for my Dovey. It wouldn't have been anyone but you. I know you'll do right by GirlChild."

Sparrow winced at the mention of the baby's name. "How a cumya like you feel about that name?"

Gentry chuckled. He was fully aware of Sparrow's feelings toward the Gullah life. He was from Mississippi and the Gullah life was a new world for him when he moved to South Carolina. The rich history of the people of the island pulled him in and he appreciated how the Singleton family strived to preserve their way of life. "You know I have no qualms with Gullah ways. I want my daughter to know where she comes from; that means knowing the Mississippi in me and the Gullah in her mama."

Sparrow was impressed at his answer. Gentry was indeed a good man. "Ha. Good answer. It'll take some getting used to for me, calling her GirlChild, but I already love her like she's my own."

"She's going to be a force to be reckoned with; did they tell you how she got here?"

"No one has told me yet. Do tell."

"She was born by the water. Not a breath in her body. Your aunts say God conjured up a storm, lightning struck my baby girl, and she drew her first breath."

Sparrow couldn't believe her ears. "Are you serious? I didn't know she wasn't breathing. Thank God she survived. Little Dove may not have been able to handle another loss."

"We wouldn't have given up though. Little Dove has always been adamant about being a mother. I'll do anything to support her and give her what she wants."

"And for that, I love you brother."

"How about I sleep in your room tonight and you sleep in Duck's old room with Little Dove and the baby?"

"You sure you wouldn't mind? I want to be as hands on as I can while I'm here."

"I wouldn't mind at all."

Gentry and Sparrow talked for a few more minutes and then went into the house to get ready for bed. It had been a long day for Sparrow and she was tired. After a long, hot shower, she quietly entered Duck's room and announced to Little Dove they would be having a slumber party.

"Gentry said I could sleep in here tonight. I hope you don't mind."

"Of course not, it'll be like old times."

Sparrow climbed into the bed next to her sister. "Have you fed her already? Changed her diaper?"

"Yes and yes. She's sound asleep for now. She'll probably wake up in a few hours for a feeding."

"Ok good. Today was such a good day. My heart is so full. I still can't believe I'm actually here."

"I can. I knew it was only a matter of time."

"You sound like Mama Maggie. You are so patient. It's been ten freaking years."

"I know, but I prayed for this day. You have to be patient when you ask God for favors."

Sparrow kissed Little Dove on the cheek. "My wise little sister. Let's get some rest. I'm exhausted."

Little Dove whispered a prayer and in no time, they were both asleep.

Chapter 8

The next morning, Sparrow woke up bright and early. She was excited about accompanying Little Dove and Gentry to the baby's doctor appointment. She eased out of bed as to not wake Little Dove; she had gotten up a few times in the middle of the night with the baby so Sparrow knew she was tired and needed to sleep in as long as possible. Sparrow tip toed over to the bassinet to find that the baby was also still sound asleep after all the fussing she had done throughout the night. Sparrow went into the bathroom to get ready for the day.

After she got dressed, she checked the time. She could hear Isaac and Isata moving about. There was a gentle knock at the door. It was Gentry coming to make sure Sparrow and Little Dove were up. He told Sparrow he would get dressed and come back when Little Dove and the baby were ready. Sparrow sat on the edge of the bed on Little Dove's side and nudged her sister to wake up. The baby started to squirm but was still asleep. Sparrow went to the dresser and picked out an outfit for the baby and Little Dove. "Dovey, what you think about this?" She held out the outfits one by one for Little Dove's approval. Little Dove didn't reply. Sparrow went back over to the bed and nudged her sister again to wake up but there was no response.

Little Dove was a heavy sleeper and the baby had worn her out. "I forgot you sleep like a log. We gotta get ready sis. We shouldn't be late to the pediatrician for the baby's first appointment." Sparrow nudged her sister one more time before she began to panic. She touched her sister forehead, and it was cool to the touch. She followed her instincts and checked her sister's pulse. A blood curdling scream escaped Sparrow's mouth, waking the baby, and sending Isaac, Isata, and Gentry rushing into the room. Isata yelled out, "What's going on in here?"

"Mama she's not breathing!"

Gentry rushed to the side of the bed and swooped Little Dove into his arms. "Dovey, baby, wake up. Wake up!"

Isaac came to Gentry's aid and checked her pulse but he could feel nothing. "Get her to the truck, now!"

Gentry raced to the truck with Little Dove in his arms and Isaac grabbed his keys and followed behind. He called out to Isata and Sparrow, "Meet us at the hospital, " before he slammed the door behind him.

Sparrow stood speechless while the baby cried out. Isata picked up the baby and consoled her; now was not the time to panic, it was the time to pray. Isata went into mother mode and packed the baby's bag as quickly as she could. She placed the baby in her car seat and handed the seat to Sparrow. She grabbed her keys and walked toward the door. Sparrow said nothing, she just followed. Isata sped to the hospital as quickly and safely as she could with the baby in the car. The hospital was thirty minutes away from their home. Sparrow was silently crying into her shirt while Isata chanted a prayer repeatedly until they got to the emergency room.

They found Isaac and Gentry in a private waiting room. No one said a word, except for Isata, chanting over and over as she rocked back and forth. Twenty minutes passed before a doctor entered the room. Isata and Isaac jumped to their feet. Gentry held the baby in one arm and Sparrow's hand in his other hand. The doctor removed his glasses and asked for Gentry. "Which of you is Mr. Parish?"

Gentry handed the baby to Sparrow. "I'm Mr. Parish. These are her parents and sister."

"I am Dr. Johnson. I am the one that saw Little Dove Parish when she was brought into the emergency room. From the information provided by an Isaac Singleton and Gentry Parish, she was brought in due to no pulse and we were informed CPR had been attempted on the drive over. Upon examination, it was apparent that she died at some time in the night or early this morning of a pulmonary embolism. I am so sorry for the loss of your loved one."

Isaac fell to his knees. Gentry punched the wall. Sparrow slid back into the chair while trying her best to keep a grip on Gentry's hand. Isata, still in mother mode, asked the tough questions. "How could this have happened?"

"Mr. Parish informed the staff of recent childbirth when she was brought in. Unfortunately, this is a very common post-delivery complication. She would have exhibited some signs prior to her passing."

"Signs like what?"

"Dizziness, chest pain, coughing, trouble breathing; the symptoms vary. Did she complain of any of those?"

Sparrow gasped. "She did, Mama; she did. I thought it was a hag again. I'm so sorry, I should have said something!"

The doctor tried to reassure them. "This is no one's fault. A pulmonary embolism can be a silent killer. Please don't blame yourself."

Isata went over to Sparrow and rubbed her back. "Thank you, Dr. Johnson. When can we see her body? I need to see my baby."

"Of course, Nurse Tanner will be in shortly and she will take you all back. Again, I'm sorry for your loss."

The doctor left the room. Isaac was inconsolable and Gentry was dumb founded, staring off into space. Isata showed a face of strength as she comforted Sparrow and took over care of the baby. When the nurse entered the room, she advised they could go back in pairs. Isata asked that Gentry be allowed to go back first alone and then Sparrow. The nurse had to physically assist Gentry with walking to the back to see Little Dove. He spent about fifteen minutes with her before he returned to the private waiting room; he just wanted to hold his daughter.

Sparrow was next. She entered the room the nurse led her to. The nurse advised she would stand outside, and that Sparrow could take as much time as she needed. Little Dove looked like the angel everyone knew her to be. Sparrow held her sister's hand. She kissed Little Dove's forehead and whispered into her ear, "I got you, forever. Girlchild will never not know love. I swear to you sis." Sparrow spent about twenty minutes with Little Dove before heading back to be with Gentry and the baby while her parents went to see Little Dove. The nurse suggested that Gentry and Sparrow head up to the children's floor to see a pediatrician since the baby was only a few days old.

The nurse's words went in one ear and out the other for Gentry. He was in a daze. Sparrow felt something in her body shift, and she went into go mode; just as she had suggested to Little Dove that she go get checked up, she knew the baby needed to be seen. "Gentry, you can stay here. I'll take the baby up and be back as soon as we're done." Gentry didn't want his daughter to leave his arms, but he eventually handed her over. Sparrow followed the nurse to the fifth floor into an examination room to wait on the pediatrician on duty. Sparrow thanked the nurse for setting everything up.

Ten minutes later, there was a knock at the door. The doctor entered the room and greeted Sparrow with a smile. "I'm Dr. Tabitha Reed. Nurse Tanner has filled me in completely. I am so sorry for the loss of your sister. I want to examine the baby to make sure she is good and healthy. I know your family would love to have that reassurance." Sparrow nervously nodded her head in agreement and lay the baby on the exam table. Dr. Reed began her exam and handled GirlChild with extreme care. She weighed the baby, checked the circumference of her head and extended her limbs. She checked GirlChild's neck, collarbone, and head as well. She talked Sparrow through the exam. They discussed known family history and the details of the baby's birth. Sparrow provided what information she could, realizing her godmother duties had started before she was ready.

"Dr. Reed, I don't know what I'm going to do without my sister but the way you have handled us today, I know that I want you to be GirlChild's doctor."

"I would love to help you navigate her care. I know this is overwhelming, but we will help you get through it. I'll send Nurse Tanner in to get an appointment schedule set up and some other details from you. Again, I'm sorry for the loss of your sister. Here's my card if you need anything, okay?"

Sparrow took the card and looked it over. She was so grateful for the pleasant experience with Dr. Reed. Despite today's turn of events, GirlChild's appointment had eased her some. After filling out paperwork to the best of her ability and setting up an appointment schedule, Nurse Tanner escorted Sparrow back downstairs where Gentry was waiting. Isaac and Isata were speaking with an administrator about next steps. They spent about four hours at the hospital before they were able to return home.

The ancestors observed from above in awe. What had just happened? Did Stepney and Sibby know this would take place? Moon silently cried into Thunder's arms. Arrow paced back and forth. Sibby and Stepney looked on in defeat. They had both known the punishment for Winter's actions would be severe and swift but neither of them could have expected that the family would have to take such a loss, this specific loss.

Little Dove was everyone's favorite, admittedly. She had always been a calming spirit and just a good person all around. Isata would often joke to the ancestors that it took her three tries to finally get it right. Little Dove could do no wrong in anyone's eyes because she always strived to treat others as she wanted to be treated. Sometimes that meant putting the needs of others before her own. She was the true definition of selfless.

Moon broke the tension and asked no one in particular, "What happens next? What do we do? Why did THIS have to happen?" Usually, Stepney would shut down any line of questioning that would offend God, but he thought that for once, the ancestors deserved the opportunity to vent and grieve. God would understand. Wouldn't He? Stepney offered the best explanation he could. "Winter's actions caused for a just decision. It was out of our control. I know everyone is taken aback and I understand it, whole heartedly. Little Dove was a bright light. But we must now move forward and guide this family, we cannot leave them helpless to tend to their grief and future alone." Arrow and Thunder nodded their heads in agreement. Moon looked defeated but she understood. Sibby said nothing as she had no words for what they all witnessed. All of them knew they were about to experience a whirlwind of emotions as the Singleton's would have to navigate grief.

When everyone made it back home, Gentry took the baby and went into the room to lay where Little Dove had lay. He wanted to smell her scent again. Isata walked around the house taking down all the mirrors. It was time to prepare for Little Dove's home going. Sparrow packed her bags to ride with Isaac onto the mainland. Isaac was going to drop her at the bus station then return to the restaurant to do an emergency shut down and deliver the news to the family that was working the morning shift. Sparrow decided she was going to go home on the first bus smoking so she could arrange to take some extended time off work and pack more clothes. She also wanted David to return with her. She planned to be back in two days.

Chapter 9

Sparrow made it back to New York the following day and took the subway home. David was still at work so she wouldn't see him until later that night. She called him to let him know what had taken place before she got on the bus. When she got home, she put down her bags and laid across the bed. She was exhausted and tired of crying. Her eyes were blood shot red and her nose was sore from constantly blowing and wiping. Although she was upset, she was excited to see David later so she decided to order take out so there would be dinner waiting on him. She called their favorite Chinese restaurant to place an order and grabbed another jacket and sunglasses before leaving to take the five-block trek to pick up the food.

After picking up the food and returning home, Sparrow took a long hot shower. As she washed away her travels and pain, she cried. She cried out toward the ceiling and her voice echoed back. She was in the shower for an hour before she got out to get dressed and lay down. In no time, she fell into a deep sleep. She had vivid dreams, dreams so real that she didn't realize she was asleep. She could see, feel, and smell Little Dove. She smiled at her sister and embraced her; she felt so real. Sparrow mumbled in her sleep, "I knew you didn't leave me." Suddenly the room began to spin, and Little Dove disappeared. Sparrow woke up to David nudging her to wake up.

"Sparrow, baby, wake up. I'm home."

Sparrow sat up in bed in confusion. "I didn't realize I had fallen asleep. What time is it?"

David kissed her cheek and checked his watch. "It's 7:30pm. I know you're tired. Thank you for ordering dinner. Can I fix you a plate?"

Sparrow shook her head. "No. I don't have an appetite. Eat without me."

David pulled her into his arms and held her tight. "I will do no such thing, my love."

Sparrow began to cry again. "Why would she leave me like this?"

David didn't have the words. He just knew he needed to be there. He rocked her back and forth until she fell asleep again.

The next morning, David and Sparrow woke up early to eat the leftover takeout for breakfast. They showered together and got dressed. David suggested they take a cab to work instead of the subway. Sparrow agreed; although she was back in the bustling city of New York, she wanted privacy and didn't want to be around a million people at the moment. They parted ways when they got to the office and Sparrow immediately stepped into a meeting with the firm's HR representative, Julie, and a managing partner, Jacob.

She explained the situation of her sister's sudden passing, the family business, and potentially taking on partial custody of her niece. Julie and Jacob were very understanding. They expressed how much they valued Sparrow and her work. A plan was drawn up for there to be coverage for Sparrow for three months while she worked out her family affairs and they would revisit at the end of the three months. Sparrow expressed her gratitude for them working with her and her situation. She loved her firm and despite the heavy workload, she planned to be there for a while, especially if David made partner.

Sparrow cleaned up her desk and gathered some personal belongings before leaving the office. She took a taxi back home and began to pack. She would be leaving the next morning to head back to South Carolina and David was coming with her. When David got off work, he picked up dinner and came home to start packing as well. They ate in silence before getting ready for bed. They had a long day ahead of them tomorrow.

The bus ride to Charleston was so long; this time around, due to multiple stops, it was twenty-one hours long. The ride gave Sparrow time to prepare David for what to expect with her family. She didn't tell him that no one knew he was white. It would be a surprise to everyone. She didn't feel the need to make a big deal about his race.

Although she didn't know the funeral arrangements yet, Sparrow assumed there would be some Gullah elements she needed to warn David about so that he wouldn't be shocked or ask too many questions. She wanted everyone to like him. She wanted them to see the good in him like she did. David processed everything he could to the best of his ability, but he didn't fully understand what he was being told. Sparrow didn't like talking about her background much and he never pressed the issue so this was all new to him. It was like he was meeting her again for the first time.

"So the funeral procession is basically a parade?"

Sparrow chuckled at how he interpreted everything she had just told him. "You could say that."

He paused before his next question as to not offend. "And the baby, GirlChild, they'll hold her over the coffin?"

"Yes; they'll pass her over the coffin so Little Dove can never enter her body."

David was dumb founded. "Do you plan on changing her name?"

"Who? GirlChild? It's wild right? But it's what Little Dove wanted; I have to honor her wishes."

"Babe, you have to think long term. What about job applications and college applications? You may want to talk to your brother-in-law about it."

Sparrow knew he was right but she didn't know how to tell him it wasn't his place to be so concerned. She wanted to do right by Little Dove. She didn't necessarily like the name either. "I'll talk to Gentry about it, eventually."

"How are you going to tell him you want the baby with us part time in New York?"

Sparrow wished he hadn't even mentioned it. She knew the news wasn't going to go over well with Gentry or her parents for that matter. They would accuse her of trying to rob GirlChild of a Gullah upbringing, but Sparrow would need for them to be realistic; there was no way she was moving back home. "Please don't mention it on this trip. They would freak out and I'm not ready to have that conversation yet. I'll lay it on them easy when I do though."

"I know these are tough decisions, but you have to have these conversations as soon as possible. You said yourself life on the island wasn't the best growing up. If you're going to take on the responsibility of this baby, you have to give her the best of everything; that means the best healthcare, childcare, and schooling."

"I know but the island is changing. The mainland is too. There is so much more development than before. Maybe she can spend 75% of the year with Gentry and my parents and 25% with us."

"It's your decision, Sparrow. I'm just here to support you."

She kissed him. "I appreciate you for being here."

The next evening, they arrived in Charleston. Duck was there to pick them up. Sparrow ran into her brother's arms. David grabbed their bags before following Sparrow to the truck. As he approached, Duck reached for the bags. "Thank you, sir. I'll take it from here." Sparrow tried her best to hold back laughter as she saw the reaction on David's confused face. "Duck, this is David. David, this is my big brother, Duck." Duck dropped the bags and his eyes doubled in size. He couldn't believe his eyes. He extended his hand and David shook it.

"It's nice to finally meet you, David. Sparrow didn't tell me you were so … tall."

David adjusted his glasses and looked Duck up and down. "Not as tall and buff as you man, you're huge."

"It's from lugging fifty-pound bags of rice around every day."

"Nice."

Sparrow thought the moment was awkward and she hoped the rest of her family wouldn't be so weird about seeing David for the first time. Duck got into the driver's seat and David held the passenger side door open for Sparrow before getting in the back seat. As David fumbled with the seatbelt, Duck started the truck up and leaned over to Sparrow and whispered, "You brought a buckra home?! They'll have your head." It took everything in Sparrow not to double over in laughter at Duck's banter. "Just drive, Duck."

An hour later, they were on Singleton Way. All of the aunts and Mama Maggie were at Isaac and Isata's. All of the cousins were at work and Isaac and the uncles were at the restaurant. Duck had taken the evening off to pick up Sparrow and David. Gentry, obviously, was on an extended leave from work and was still staying with Isaac and Isata so they could help with the baby. Duck pulled into the driveway and honked the horn twice. Isata came outside to greet them and the look on her face was priceless. She yelled out, "Oh my Lord!" This prompted the aunts and Mama Maggie to come out onto the porch.

Sparrow was so embarrassed. David didn't seem to understand

what the commotion was about and figured everyone was just happy to see Sparrow again. Duck was tickled at their reaction. Duck grabbed their bags and suggested David follow him through the crowd into the house so he could show David where they would be sleeping. Sparrow stayed behind and prepared to be interrogated by the women folk.

Ola laid into her, "You brought a buckra here?"

Isata asked, "That's David?"

Esther chimed in, "All this time he was white and you said nothing?"

Lille offered her two cents. "At least he's an established white man. He's too pale though."

Mama Maggie put her hand up to silence them all. "We will treat our guest with respect. Now, quiet before he hears you."

She grabbed Sparrow by the arm and led her into the living room. Sparrow thought to herself how Mama Maggie was always coming to her rescue. In this case, she was grateful. Isata brought some tea into the living room. There was much to be said but they sat in silence for a few moments sipping their tea before Sparrow broke the ice.

"So, how is the funeral planning going? Do I need to do anything?"

Isata updated her. "Gentry and I took care of everything. It will be beautiful. The funeral is to be in two days."

"Great. How has Gentry been?"

Mama Maggie spoke first. "He barely leaves that room. Poor thang. He been sleeping in the chair watching over GirlChild. He won't even let anyone make the bed. It's been unmade since the morning Little Dove left us."

Sparrow processed her grandmother's words. *Little Dove left us. She's gone.* Sparrow couldn't believe this was real. She was living in a nightmare. How was she supposed to go on without her baby sister? Out of nowhere, the emotions rushed up her throat like vomit and she began to shriek and cry. Ola and Isata ran to her side, rubbing her back. Sparrow shook them both off and ran out of the house. No one could console her right now. There was nothing anyone could say to make her process what was happening.

She ran until she got to the water. She hadn't been near the water since she was a teenager. She let out a scream and asked, "Why?" She didn't know who she was talking to or that she even wanted to be heard; she just knew she needed to release the pain. Sparrow got into the fetal position, holding her knees to her chest. She rocked back and forth to comfort herself and for the first time in ages, she prayed.

The ancestors could not believe their ears. Sparrow's scream summoned them. They gathered on a cloud as she cried out and prayed. Moon's mood changed instantly; she was so elated to witness such a momentous occasion. "Finally, she needs us. She wants our help." Stepney called a meeting to order. "Despite our feelings on the death of Little Dove, God always has a plan. As you can see, it's falling together naturally. Sparrow hasn't called out to us in years. She is hurting and we need to guide her through this journey of grief." Sibby continued, "it's also time the family be open with her about what's going on with the land. This is Sparrow's purpose. She is destined to save our way of life from destruction." Arrow agreed. "I am ready for the task. I believe we are all ready to do what needs to be done." Thunder stood in allegiance. "For Little Dove."

The ancestors dispersed but Moon stayed behind. She wanted to watch over Sparrow a little longer. Moon conjured up a warm wind to blow around Sparrow; a way of letting Sparrow know her prayers had been heard. Sparrow eventually stopped crying and talked herself down. Moon whispered, "I got you little one."

Chapter 10

Later that night, Sparrow lay next to David in silence. He snored lightly while she starred at the ceiling. It was only 9:00 pm but they were both tired from the bus ride. Sparrow carefully climbed out of bed as to not wake David. She walked across the hall to Duck's old bedroom and knocked gently. There was no answer. She knocked again and heard Gentry call out. She entered the room and Gentry was sitting in the chair next to the baby's bassinet. Just as Mama Maggie had revealed, Sparrow observed that the bed was not made.

She motioned toward the bed for Gentry's permission for her to sit down. He nodded his head that it was okay. They sat quietly for a moment before either of them spoke. Sparrow wanted more details about the funeral arrangements.

"I just wanted to know if you needed me to do anything for the funeral. I don't really know what's going on at this point."

"You don't have to lift a finger. Little Dove and I both had burial policies. It's taken care of; your mother and I agreed we would start with a brief viewing of the body before we march to the cemetery for a graveside burial."

Sparrow was relieved to hear the plans. "I'll be honest, I'm glad to hear it will be brief. I don't think I can sit in a church house for hours hearing about how beautiful my sister's life was because she isn't here anymore."

"I agree. That was my line of thinking as well. I understand there are Gullah traditions, but I don't want to dwell on the fact that she's gone. I want to focus on what she left behind, and that's our daughter."

"I agree that is for the best. GirlChild needs us now more than ever. Did mama talk to you about them passing the baby over the grave?"

"She did. I don't have an issue with it. But seeing as she has this gray patch of hair, I'm pretty sure she's been here before; I doubt Little Dove could come back through GirlChild. I understand it's a tradition though."

"I didn't even think about that; the gray patch of hair. She's going to be just as wise as her mother."

"I got to meet your David. A buckra huh?"

Sparrow chuckled. "I honestly didn't know how to tell the family. I didn't think it would be such a big deal."

"Hey, you love who you love. Your family embraced me with open arms when Little Dove first brought me home. They made feel so welcome. I'm sure they will come around with David as well."

"I hope so. He's my person."

Gentry and Sparrow talked for another hour before the baby woke up fussing. Sparrow went into the kitchen for a bottle and brought it back to Gentry before she returned to her old bedroom. David was still sound asleep. She didn't feel sleepy even though her body was tired. She lay there as her thoughts raced. She tried to redirect her thoughts to something positive.

Isaac and Isata invited David to come to the restaurant the next day for breakfast and to see the day-to-day operations. Sparrow appreciated their effort in making David feel welcome. For some reason, even though they had been together for years, Sparrow felt the need to impress David on this trip. She didn't want him to think her family was some ass backwards, broken English speaking people. The Singletons were a proud, hardworking family and when he saw how they ran the restaurant, he would certainly agree or at least she hoped he would.

The house was in motion bright and early the next morning. Isaac and Isata sat in the kitchen drinking coffee while they waited on Sparrow and David to finish getting dressed. It was 5:00 am. Gentry was up fixing a bottle for GirlChild. Isata whipped up a small breakfast and left the plate out for him to eat when he was settled after feeding the baby. Isaac, Isata, Sparrow, and David were out the house by 5:15am and headed to the restaurant. Isaac's brother's, Elijah, James, John, and Daniel were already there prepping for the 6:00 am crowd.

Isaac parked in the back so they could go in through the kitchen. Isata put on an apron and began to fix a meal for Sparrow and David. Isaac headed into the office to look over some paperwork. Sparrow's cousins, August, June, and Isabella were in the dining area getting silverware together. August would manage the register and host desk and June and Isabella would serve. Sparrow picked a table near the kitchen so she and David would be out of the way.

Moments later, Isata brought out two plates of fried fish, grits, and biscuits for Sparrow and David. David grabbed his fork to dig in but before he could take a bite, Isata cleared her throat and glared at Sparrow. Sparrow took away David's fork and took his hands into hers and gave him a look that said, 'just go with it.' Isata prayed over their food. They said "Amen" in unison. Isata returned to the kitchen to help. David looked at Sparrow in confusion.

"What was that? Since when do you pray?"

"Not often but when you're in the presence of Gullah people, you must pray."

David dug into the grits and moaned in satisfaction. "For these grits, I'll pray anytime."

Sparrow laughed. "I know how to fix those you know; I'll have to start cooking more."

David bit into the crispy fish. "Mmm, you definitely should. You didn't tell me the food would be this good."

Sparrow picked at her food. David noticed she wasn't eating. He put down his fork and wiped his mouth with a napkin. He grabbed Sparrow's hand.

"What's wrong?"

"I'm just thinking about if I'm ready for tomorrow."

"How could you possibly be ready for your sister's funeral?"

"I know, I know. It's just, it's supposed to be a homegoing, a celebration. I don't want to damper the mood with all that crying and screaming while Mama and Daddy are holding their heads high."

"I may not understand your culture fully yet, but I think funerals are for crying babe. If you need to cry, I'll be right there with you."

"I hate your first time in South Carolina had to be for this reason. I wish you could have met Little Dove. It's my fault this happened. I should have come home sooner."

"Whoa, whoa; this isn't your fault. You're just one person. What could you have possibly done?"

"I could have made her have a more orthodox birthing experience. She would have had better care. The doctors would have been able to see his coming and prevent it. She was coughing and complaining of chest pain, and I thought it was a fucking hag."

David didn't even want to know what a hag was; he just knew he needed to comfort Sparrow. "Listen to me, there is nothing you could have done. Little Dove made her own decision about how she wanted to bring her child into this world. Now eat something."

Sparrow considered whether David was right. If she had been

home, what could she have done? She didn't even know Little Dove was pregnant. In hindsight, she held some resentment toward Ola but she didn't want to speak on it aloud. It would only create conflict.

Ola was the family's medicine woman, and it was rare she recommended modern medicine, especially since the nearest hospital was thirty minutes away. Sparrow believed Ola should have sent Little Dove to the hospital after the birth of the baby. All the signs were there: previous miscarriages and stillbirths, the premature birth of GirlChild, postpartum symptoms of extreme exhaustion, chest pain, and coughing spells; Little Dove could barely walk on her own. Sparrow decided she would put her concerns with Ola's care of Little Dove on the back burner. With the funeral coming up, the last thing the family needed to be doing was arguing.

Sparrow and David continued their breakfast and people watched as customers rolled in. There was a large crowd of sit ins and even more to-go orders. August, June, and Isabella handled everyone flawlessly and with care. Isaac came from the kitchen and suggested David shadow him. David gladly followed Isaac into the kitchen. He was excited to see the ins and outs of Singleton's Kitchen. From what he observed, business was great, and they had a loyal customer base. He couldn't believe Sparrow came from such a successful family. She acted like she spent her younger years oppressed. Granted, there wasn't much to do on the island, but David could see the potential in the mainland.

After the lunch hour, August locked the front door and flipped the open sign over to show they were closed. She taped an announcement in the door window that they would be closed for the rest of the week in honor of Little Dove. There were funeral details listed in the event any customers wanted to come. Sparrow helped June and Isabella clean the dining area while August count down the register for deposits and did paperwork. In the kitchen, David helped the

Singleton men and Isata clean up. They needed the space clear and clean so they could prep the feast for tomorrow. They would prep everything, and trusted members of the church would come in and cook so the family didn't have to worry about it.

Isata announced she would be taking the truck to go to the funeral home for about an hour. She suggested that Sparrow come along. Sparrow hadn't seen her sister's body since the hospital. She grabbed her purse and followed Isata out the back door. On the way to the funeral home, they picked up Duck from his home. They rode in silence; no one knew what to say. They pulled into the parking lot of Carter's Funeral Home. They were greeted by the owner, one of their church members, James Carter IV. He welcomed them in and took them directly to see Little Dove. He drew the curtains in the room to let in sunlight.

Isata, Duck, and Sparrow gasped as sunlight entered the room and Little Dove could be seen. She lay beautifully in a white dress. Her arms, at her side. Her hair in a soft top bun like she always wore it. Her cinnamon skin glistened in the sunlight. She looked to be asleep. Duck stepped forward and grabbed his little sister's hand.

"You look like the first day of Spring, I miss you already Little Dove."

Sparrow joined him. "She looks like an angel."

Isata looked her daughter over and planted a cheek on her forehead. "I have to go make some final touches with Mr. Carter. I'll only be a minute then we can leave. I'll be right back."

Sparrow tried to hold back her tears, but it was not easy. Duck held her in his arms and hummed a tune to calm her down. Once she was able to calm herself down, Sparrow questioned her brother.

"Do you think if I had come home sooner this wouldn't have happened?"

Duck was shocked at what he was hearing. "Huh? There's no way you could have known. You didn't even know she was pregnant."

"I know, but I could have made sure she was getting the proper care had I known. When I first got here, I could sense something was wrong. Te Ola should have done more."

Duck threw up his hands. "Slow down Sparrow, there is no one to blame. No one could have known we would lose her like this. Don't think negatively. Te Ola birthed all three of us. She's taken care of us since we were babies. She has never had anything but our best interest at heart."

"You think I'm jumping the gun."

"You are jumping the gun. Please don't mention this in front of mama or the aunts. You would raise hell and that's the last thing we need."

"Okay, I won't."

"Sparrow, promise me."

"I promise."

Isata returned a few moments later. She kissed Little Dove once more before she announced they were leaving. They dropped Duck back off at home before heading back to the restaurant. There was much to be done.

Sibby and Moon sat together and watched from above. They were both concerned about Sparrow's accusations. Ola was led by the ancestors. She could not practice medicine without their guidance and knowledge from previous family members. Sibby was angry.

"Sparrow is proving to still be the problem child we all know her to be. How could she say such things about Ola?"

Moon disagreed. "I think her concerns are valid; just wrong. She will realize in time that Ola's intentions in her care of Little Dove were pure. There is no one to blame, she's just grieving."

"You are always placing your faith in these young people. First Winter and now Sparrow."

"They are our future. We must stand by them no matter what; it is our job to guide them."

"Well, you see where standing by Winter has gotten us. It would do you some good not to trust so easily. Sparrow is a hot head."

Moon sighed. "I cannot lose faith just because of what Winter did. I believe whole heartedly Sparrow will come around."

Sibby rolled her eyes. "Let's hope so."

Chapter 11

The day had come; Little Dove's homegoing. The Singleton family woke up bright and early. They needed to be at the church by 8:45am. The viewing would be from 9:00am until 10:30 am before they marched half a mile to the cemetery. They would march back to the church to fellowship and eat after the burial.

Sparrow hurried to get dressed so she could dress the baby while Gentry got ready. She knocked and entered Duck's old room. GirlChild was finishing a bottle. Gentry handed her over and left the room to go to the hall bathroom and get ready for the day. Sparrow burped GirlChild before placing her back in the bassinet. She went through the dresser drawers before deciding on a cute, white dress. She wanted GirlChild and Little Dove to match.

Sparrow dressed the baby and fixed her bag for the day. Once she was done, she lay the baby in the middle of the bed and lay next to her. The baby cooed and kicked. "Today's the big day, GirlChild. On one hand, I wish you were older and understood what was going on and on the other hand, I'm glad you're still a baby. Losing your mother is the greatest pain I've had to endure thus far. I can't imagine how it's going to be when you're older and you see how great of a person she was." Sparrow rambled on to GirlChild. "How do you feel about your name? Do you think we should change it? If you came to live in New York, you would have to at the very least have a nickname." Sparrow rolled over and looked into GirlChild's eyes. In her niece, she could see Little Dove; she could see the future.

Isata interrupted and entered the room. "Everyone is ready to go. I'll grab her car seat." Sparrow sat up and picked up the baby before grabbing the baby's bag. She was going to ride with Gentry and David. She strapped GirlChild in the car seat and they were on their way to the mainland to the church.

The Singleton family filled in the first few pews of the church. Members of the community started to come in at 9:00 am on the dot. They greeted the family before viewing Little Dove's body and then took a seat. David whispered to Sparrow how he couldn't believe there were so many people. He had never been to such a large funeral. Sparrow told him it was just a sign of how much Little Dove meant to everyone.

At 10:30 am, Mr. Carter and Reverend Hoyt provided instructions on how the funeral procession would take place. The family would be at the front behind the drummer and everyone else would follow. They lined up to exit the church. The drummer hit the drum twice to get everyone's attention and then led them out into the street as they walked the half mile to get to the cemetery. The drummer banged the drum as they walked through the community to announce the death of Little Dove. Some people came out of their homes and businesses to join the procession.

When they arrived at the burial plot, everyone gathered around in a circle as Mama Maggie, Isaac, Isata, Duck, Sparrow, and Gentry were seated in front of the grave site. Ola held the baby and stood next to Gentry's chair. David stood behind Sparrow. Reverend Hoyt raised his hand and the chatter amongst everyone stopped. He promised that at the request of the family, his sermon would be short and sweet so they could get back to the church to celebrate. He began.

"We gather here today on the Lord's day to celebrate the life of an exceptional young woman, Little Dove Parish. Although her time with us has come to an end, we thank God for the opportunity to shine a light on all she contributed to our lives during her time on this earth. Today, we recognize a true Proverbs 31 woman. She was a daughter, sister, wife, mother, and friend. In all of these roles, the only language she spoke was one of kindness. She was wise beyond her years and her approach to trials and tribulations is one that we could all fashion after.

Now, I have known Little Dove since she was a baby. Isaac and Isata had those children in church from day one. Little Dove was a special something. From the day she understood the word, she allowed her faith to lead her in everything she did. She treated others the way she wanted to be treated. She left a mark on every person she came across. Little Dove was a true beacon of light.

I think most of us within the community knew about her struggles with fertility. I have gotten permission from the family to acknowledge this as a way for you all to see her unwavering faith in God. After every loss, I would summon Little Dove and we would speak about the turmoil she endured time and time again. Do you know she never complained? Not once. She believed everything happened for a reason and that God would bless her when it was her time to bring a child to full term. As my witness, you see the work of God today in the presence of her daughter, GirlChild.

As we stand here today, let us commit to carrying forward the same attitude Little Dove had towards life. She represented love, faith, and community. Her love knew no bounds, her faith was unwavering, and her commitment to community was strong. Let's mirror that in our day -to-day life in her honor. Let us also pray that GirlChild follows in her mother's footsteps.

I know this won't be easy for those that loved her most. Let us draw comfort in the words of Revelation 21:4, "And God shall wipe away all tears from their eyes; and there shall be no more death, neither sorrow, nor crying, neither shall there be any more pain: for the former things are passed away." For every death, there is new life. I know best that Little Dove would want us to surround Gentry and GirlChild with love. It is time to love thy neighbor.

As I close out, let us remember that although Little Dove is no longer with us physically, her presence is undoubtedly with us. We carry her in the way we treat one another; we carry her in our hearts. The impact she had will carry on in that of her daughter; her birth being a reminder to never give up on God's promise. We pray for the healing of the Parish and Singleton family. We also pray for the healing of this community. May her soul rest in eternal peace. Amen."

In unison, the congregation agreed, "Amen." Reverend Hoyt motioned for the immediate family to stand. The funeral home staff passed out personal items of Little Dove's from a sweetgrass basket. Gentry was given a bouquet of palmetto roses. They each took turns tossing items into the open grave. Ola stepped forward and passed GirlChild to Reverend Hoyt. It was time to pass her over the grave. Isaac stood on the other side to receive his granddaughter. Gentry declined to participate as it wasn't his custom. Reverend Hoyt gently unwrapped the baby from her blanket and carefully passed her over the grave to Isaac.

After everyone paid their respects, they marched back to the church for fellowship. A feast was waiting for them in the dining hall of the church. Church members served the family first and then everyone else lined up to get a plate. David and Sparrow sat across from one another at the family table. David had so many questions and he couldn't resist seizing the moment.

"How are you feeling, Sparrow?"

"As good as I can be I guess."

"Are you satisfied with how the service went?"

"I am. Everything was beautiful."

"Are all funerals like this down here?"

"What do you mean?"

"Marching to the cemetery. Why didn't we take a hearse? And why did you guys put that stuff in the grave? Oh, and why was the baby passed over the grave? Don't you think that's a bit dangerous?"

Sparrow found his curiosity hilarious, but Duck was sitting next to them and he overheard. He didn't find it to be funny one bit. "These are Gullah customs. It would do Sparrow some good to educate you instead of laughing." He pushed his chair back and left the table.

David was embarrassed. "I'm sorry. I didn't mean anything by it. I was just curious."

Sparrow reached across the table and took his hand into hers. "It's okay, Duck is just emotional about today's events. He didn't mean anything by it. Let's talk about this later, okay?"

David nodded his head and pulled his hand away. The damage was done; Duck was pissed and David wasn't sure how he could recover.

After they finished fellowshipping, the Singleton family returned home. They were all tired. They lounged around the house and napped for a few hours. Isata surveyed the house when everyone woke up and concluded that there was no need to cook dinner because everyone was still stuffed from the repast. Isata retired to her bedroom early to meditate and pray. Isaac joined her.

Sparrow suggested she and David have a cup of tea on the porch. They agreed they weren't ready for bed yet. They sat in rocking chairs and watched the sun set. Since they were alone, Sparrow figured it was a better time to educate David on her culture. In all the years they had known one another, he didn't ask, and she didn't tell. He took her at her word when she said she was just a girl from South Carolina. He saw no reason to pry.

"David, do you want to continue our conversation from earlier?"

"Only if you're comfortable; I really didn't mean to offend."

"I know you didn't. Duck is right, it's my fault. You should know more about Gullah culture. It's a part of me whether I like it or not."

"Well, for starters, what is Gullah culture? I thought you were African American."

Sparrow chuckled. "Oh my, where do I even start? In short, I am African American, but my people are Gullah. We are descendants of enslaved Africans that worked the rice, indigo, and cotton plantations on the sea islands. Gullah is an African creole language. My paternal ancestors were brought through the port of Charleston from West Africa. South Carolina used to be called the Rice Coast; that's why we thrive in selling rice at the restaurant. We are one of the few families that still farm rice."

"So, your Mama Maggie isn't speaking broken English, it's actually a language?"

Sparrow looked around to make sure they were still alone. If anyone heard David call their tongue broken English, they would have a fit. "Never call it broken English; it's offensive. But yes, it's actually a language."

"Why don't you speak it?"

"I choose not to; growing up, kids at the academy on the mainland that weren't Gullah made fun of me. I haven't spoken it in years. Plus, I'm a professional, career woman, imagine me speaking in Gullah at work."

"Ahh, I see. Interesting. Who knew there was more to you? I just thought you were a southerner."

"I should have educated you sooner."

Sparrow and David spent the rest of the evening talking about her childhood. She spoke of memories of Little Dove. She even told him about the time she confronted the hag that had been riding her sister. David couldn't believe his ears. He wasn't a big believer, although he had been raised Catholic, so hearing Sparrow talk about God, spirits, and hags was mind blowing. David thought about how Sparrow would be spending the next three months home while he would have to return to New York next week to get back to work. David tried to hide the concern on his face as he wondered if her reconnection with her roots would change her; he wondered who she would be the next time they saw one another.

Chapter 12

The next few days dragged on. The restaurant was going to be closed for a week to give the family time to gather their bearings. In the meantime, the Singleton men worked in the field. Sparrow got to spend some time with her cousins. David got to know Duck and Gentry better.

One night, Duck took Gentry and David to a bar on the mainland to get some beer and listen to some live music. They went to the Shake Shack; a hole in the wall. The Jones Brothers Band was performing with Lady Beverly at the forefront. They sat at a table in the back near the bar. Duck was familiar with the server, so she came over right away and took their orders.

Lady Beverly crooned, and her voice filled the place and bounced off the walls. David had never heard such a dominant voice. He was drawn in immediately. Duck laughed as he watched David look on in awe. Gentry swirled the ice cubes in his whiskey around. He was far removed from what was going on around him.

Duck waited until the band's first set was over to strike up a conversation. He knew he owed David an apology for snapping at the repast. He invited David out with the intent of extending an olive branch. He could only imagine how awkward David felt being amongst so many black people and witnessing cultural customs he had never seen before.

"I gotta say David, you're cool with me man. I gotta apologize for the way I reacted the other day. I meant no harm. I was more frustrated with Sparrow than anything."

"It's all good man. I appreciate the apology."

Duck continued. "You see, it was just shocking to see you, you know; Sparrow never told us you were white."

David was caught off guard, but he didn't want to reveal his hand. "It's not a big deal man, I promise."

Gentry threw back the shot of whiskey and joined the conversation. "I know what it's like being an outsider. I moved here from Mississippi. It can be a culture shock at first but it's a beautiful thing all in all."

David appreciated Gentry opening up to him. He could tell Gentry's mind was really elsewhere. "I thought you were a native. I couldn't even tell. You blend in so well with the family."

Duck expressed his frustration once more. "See, that's what I mean. Sparrow ain't tell you no details about any of us?"

David sensed Duck wasn't over the situation like he claimed to be. "Sparrow is a strong woman. She's very guarded. It took me a while to crack her, she's really private. I'm still learning about her."

Gentry was a light weight and the shot of whiskey had given him liquid courage to say what both he and Duck were thinking. "You don't see anything wrong with that? You guys have been together since college and you're still on a surface level with her; shouldn't you know more?"

Before David could answer, the band started back up. He silently thanked God for saving him from the interrogation. He also realized that Gentry and Duck were right, but he wouldn't throw Sparrow under the bus and admit that to them. David definitely planned on having a private conversation with Sparrow. He wanted to know who he was lying next to every night.

As the night continued, so did the drinks and music. Before long, Duck was flirting with the server and David was dancing with Lady Beverly. Gentry was on stage playing an air guitar next to the band. They were suddenly the life of the party. After the band's last set, they all sat down to have one last round of drinks. It was apparent they were nearly drunk. A DJ began playing music while the band broke down their equipment.

David was in a good mood. He leaned onto Duck. "Thank you for having me out man. I haven't had a night like this since college!"

Duck could see that David was finally more relaxed. "I'm glad to hear it man. Ya'll don't have spots like this back in New York?"

"If we do, I've never been. I don't really get out a lot. I work crazy hours, so does your sister. I'm on track to be partner at the firm."

Gentry leaned in. "Man that's great! I've always wanted to visit New York. Maybe Duck and I can come visit one day and you show us around."

"Aww man, I'd love that. I guess you'll be coming up to New York often anyway to visit the baby."

Gentry was suddenly sober. "Visit the baby?"

"Yea, GirlChild. You'll probably be doing a lot of commuting once we start to keep her."

Gentry lurched across the table and grabbed David by the collar. Both of their chairs fell to the ground. Gentry's eyes were blood shot red. Duck didn't comprehend what was going on but realized everyone was looking so he tried to calm Gentry down. Gentry yelled at David.

"You and Sparrow trying to take my baby away from me? My GirlChild?"

David stuttered getting his words out. "No man! Be cool. I thought you guys were splitting custody! I don't even know what I'm talking about man, forget I said anything!"

"My daughter ain't leaving the state without my permission and I damn sure ain't sharing custody with a woman that lay with a buckra that don't know nothing about nothing!" Gentry released David and stormed off to the parking lot.

Duck went after Gentry. David tried to regain his composure. Once again, he had been embarrassed for speaking out of turn. He blamed Sparrow. The night they sat on the porch and talked, she promised she would have a conversation with Gentry about sharing custody of GirlChild; she said she would do it the next day. By Gentry's actions, it was apparent a conversation never took place. Now David was fuming. He grabbed his jacket and got up to leave but the server called out to him, "Hey! Somebody gotta cover the tab!" David walked over to the bar and smacked down a hundred-dollar bill.

Duck drove back to Singleton Way with the radio blasting to drown out their thoughts. When they got to the house, Gentry went straight to Duck's old bedroom and slammed the door. The baby was sleeping in Isaac and Isata's room for the night. Duck decided he was too tired to drive back home and would crash on the couch in the living room. Before David retreated to the bedroom, Duck offered some words of advice. "I wouldn't harp on it tonight. You'll only wake the house. Cool off first and talk about it tomorrow."

David took heed of Duck's words. He entered the bedroom quietly so not to wake Sparrow, but she stirred anyway. Duck changed into some pajamas and joined her in bed. She rolled over and asked him how the night had been. David only offered, "We're going to a hotel tomorrow and it's not up for discussion." Sparrow spent the rest of the night trying to coax an explanation out of David, but he wouldn't budge.

The next morning, David and Sparrow packed their bags. Sparrow explained to her parents that they needed some alone time but that she would be back after David left to return to New York. They caught a ride to Charleston with Duck and checked into a hotel. Once they were settled, Sparrow ordered room service as they hadn't had breakfast yet. David was quiet the entire time. He was still recovering from a whiskey-filled night.

Once the food arrived, they sat at the table to partake. Sparrow reached for David's hands to say grace, but he snatched his hands back and glared at her. "Why pray when you don't even believe it?" Sparrow was taken aback. *What had gotten into him?*

"What is the problem, David? You come into my parents' house drunk and tell me we're moving to a hotel but that you won't talk about why. Now you're offended I want to pray over the food?"

"Oh, I'm not offended, I'm embarrassed!"

"Embarrassed about what?"

"Didn't you tell me you were going to talk to Gentry about having partial custody of the baby?"

Sparrow hesitated. "Yes."

"Did you do it?"

"No, I hadn't gotten around to it yet."

"Because of your fear of facing conflict, I put my foot in my mouth last night! Gentry wasn't too happy with me and he sure as hell isn't pleased with you right now."

"What did you say to him?"

"I said he would be spending a lot of time visiting New York with us keeping the baby and all. He thinks you're trying to take her away from him. And he called me a buckra, what the hell is that?"

"A buckra is a white man."

"Why didn't you tell your family I was white? Are you ashamed of me or something?"

"Of course not! I just didn't think it was a big deal."

"Well, from what I'm gathering, in your culture it's a pretty big fucking deal. You should have been more forthcoming."

"I know. I'm sorry, David. I just don't know how to face my family sometimes."

"Gentry almost choked me out last night. You need to speak with him. He needs to know your intentions."

"What intentions? Everything is ruined now. There's no way he's going to let me move GirlChild to New York when she's of age."

"Stop calling her that, call her something else. I cringe every time I hear it."

"GirlChild? It's her name David. Get used to it."

"You should discuss changing it when you talk to Gentry. How will she ever get a job with a name like that?"

Sparrow was growing agitated although David was right. She needed to speak with Gentry to make her intentions known and clear the air. Gentry would have to see the bigger picture. GirlChild would have a better future in New York, and it wasn't too late to change her name, she wasn't even a month old yet. It wasn't like she answered to the name. "I'll talk to him."

They spent the afternoon laying around watching tv. David was in and out of sleep, trying to get rid of his hangover. Sparrow called Duck and asked him to pick her up and drop her off at the restaurant. She needed to get out of the stuffy hotel room and talk to Isata. She felt like the room was closing in on her. Duck arrived an hour later. David stayed behind to get some more rest.

Sparrow wasted no time tearing into Duck when she got into the truck. "Why did you get David drunk last night?"

Duck laughed. "I am not responsible for the actions of a grown man. Plus, we had a good time until we didn't."

"You should've done something. Why would you let Gentry

put his hands on David?"

"Like I said, I can't control grown ass men Sparrow. David should have kept his mouth closed. Although, he was speaking based on your lack of words and actions."

"So you're blaming me?"

Duck threw up his hands before returning them to the wheel. "Hey, you're the one that brought a buckra here without educating him on your background and family. He has so many unanswered questions. Why were you even hiding who we are?"

"I wasn't hiding. I just don't see the need to broadcast that I'm Gullah. I worked hard to get where I am today. Do you think I would be where I am speaking broken English and telling people I can see hags and feel spirits?"

Duck slammed on the brakes and pulled the truck over. "How dare you speak about our culture that way! You wouldn't be who you are today without it! Everyone says how strong willed you are on your own, but you wouldn't be who you are today without our upbringing."

Sparrow knew she had gone too far. All she could do was apologize and sink back into the seat. "I'm sorry."

They rode in silence the rest of the way. Duck was pissed and Sparrow was indifferent. He dropped her off at the restaurant and continued on to the rice field. Isaac and Isata decided to open the restaurant earlier than anticipated. They were tired of sitting around at home in their grief. Once news spread that the restaurant was back open, people flocked to Singleton's Kitchen. The parking lot was full and there was a tour bus out back. Sparrow arrived just in time for the extended lunch hour.

The ancestors were meeting. Stepney was fuming. Sibby was perturbed as well. After everything that happened the night before and just now, Moon knew she couldn't defend Sparrow's words. Thunder wasn't surprised at Sparrow's actions. Arrow didn't know what to think of all of it. Stepney roared so loud it began raining from the cloud they were sitting on. "Broken English? How dare she! Sparrow has proven time and time again to be an ungrateful, entitled brat!"

Sibby sighed. She was so tired of Sparrow's self-hate. "What are we going to do with her? She's too far gone. No one can make her love herself; she has to want to do the work."

Moon interjected, trying to remain positive. "Maybe the time she spends here for the next few months will turn her around. I don't like that David. He seems like an oppressor; questioning the baby's name like that?"

Arrow agreed. "I don't like him either, damn buckra. What GirlChild ever do to him?"

Thunder tried to speak with reason. "In his defense, Sparrow hasn't been very open with him about who she is and where she comes from. She's ashamed."

They all agreed. Sparrow was ashamed and had been since she was a child. The ancestors had watched her dwell in years of self-hate and had no idea how to reverse it.

Chapter 13

The extended lunch hour was finally over, and the last customer was gone. It began raining but the sun was still out. Isata pulled Sparrow to the side to talk. She could tell something was wrong. They sat at a table near the front of the restaurant away from the rest of the family.

Isata pulled Sparrow's hands into hers and looked into her daughter's eyes. "Wha goin on?" Sparrow turned to the window to hide hear tears, but Isata grabbed her face. "Look ya." Sparrow looked back to her mother and wiped her tears.

"Mama, no Gullah, please."

"Ok, no Gullah but no lies either. Tell me what's going on with you."

"I don't even know where to begin."

"For starters, tell me why you and David are really at a hotel."

Sparrow hesitated. "David and Gentry had an argument last night. David thought it would be awkward to be in the house with Gentry."

Isata was shocked. "An argument about what?"

"David let it slip that I was going to propose having partial custody of the baby and moving her to New York when she's of age."

Isata sighed out of frustration. "You know Gentry, Isaac, and I wouldn't let Little Dove's only child go up to that devilish land you live in. Just because you hate it here doesn't mean GirlChild will; you have always had it in your head that the rest of the world is better than us. Why are you so ashamed of who you are? I didn't raise you to be that way."

Sparrow was tired of being chastised by everyone. "I'm tired of people telling me what I think! I was not meant to live on this ass backwards island. I want more out of life than working in a restaurant and slaving in a rice field. I want to leave a legacy behind."

Isata was enraged. "What is legacy without family? You up there in New York alone; living with an oppressor. Working crazy hours and not living life."

"I am working toward something! And David is not an oppressor, he's a good man."

"If he's such a good man, why did you wait so long to bring him down? Why didn't you tell us he was white?"

"Because that doesn't matter!"

Their shouting match caught the attention of the family. August walked over and grabbed Sparrow. She suggested Sparrow ride with her to take Mama Maggie some food. Sparrow didn't say a word to Isata before leaving out the back door.

On the ride to Mama Maggie's, August tried to comfort Sparrow. They used to be so close when they were younger but Sparrow's move to New York changed all of that. Sparrow became too busy, and the family practically begged her to come home, but she never did until the birth of GirlChild. Sparrow used to confide in August all the time. August hoped today would be no different.

"Sparrow, are you okay?"

"I'm stressed out. I didn't know coming home would stir up so many unresolved issues."

"Seriously? You've been gone for ten years; something was bound to happen. Don't be naïve."

"I guess you're right. I'm just tired, August. I'm tired of arguing about the same thing over and over again. Sure, I haven't been home in a while, but I always kept in touch."

"We needed you, physically."

"Needed me how? Everything seems to be running smooth here without me. The restaurant and rice field are successful. Everyone seems happy."

"We needed you in more ways than one and you haven't been present. There were so many times I wanted to call on you to come down and celebrate a milestone with me. All those miscarriages Little Dove endured; I know she would have loved to have her sister by her side."

Sparrow paused to think about what August was saying. She realized she hadn't been dependable. Little Dove needed her, and she failed her time and time again. She began crying. August rubbed her back. Sparrow eventually calmed down and dried her eyes; she had nothing else to say on the matter for now. When they pulled into Mama Maggie's driveway, she checked her eyes to make sure they were no longer red. She put on a smile; she didn't need Mama Maggie questioning her too.

As she got out of the car, Sparrow noticed a Mercedes Benz parked in front of the house. She asked August whose car it was, and August sucked her teeth and rolled her eyes. "Probably another one of those leeches from Sunset Corp." Sparrow was confused. As they approached the porch, Mama Maggie was walking a young man out. He was about six feet tall with skin the color of licorice. Sparrow tried not to blush as she observed how handsome he was. In passing, he tipped his hat to Sparrow and August. "Ladies." He turned to Mama Maggie once more before getting into the car. "Ms. Singleton, I do hope you consider my offer."

August and Sparrow were in awe at this man. The way he dressed, walked and talked; he had swagger. August waited until he was in the car. "Mama Maggie, who is that?" Mama Maggie shushed her and ushered August and Sparrow into the house. "Hush gal before he hears you." The girls giggled and followed their grandmother into the dining room.

Sparrow inhaled the man's cologne that had been floating in the air. "Ooo Mama Maggie, it smell like a man in here." August and Mama Maggie laughed. August went into the kitchen to warm up Mama Maggie's food. Sparrow was curious. "Who was that?"

"One of them attorneys from Sunset Corp."

"Sunset Corp?"

August yelled from the kitchen. "They wanna buy the family land!"

Sparrow suddenly felt sick to the stomach. "They wanna do what?"

Mama Maggie continued. "They wanna buy this twenty-five acres we got here. They been approaching me and other people for the past year and a half. They want to build more resorts and stuff."

Sparrow felt herself panicking. "But you're not going to let them, right?"

"I'll try my best. We'll see."

"Mama Maggie, that's not good enough. Why didn't anyone tell me about this?"

"What were you going to do from New York?"

"I don't know. I could have found someone to help, a colleague that specializes in this type of thing."

August provided some detail as she re-entered the dining room with Mama Maggie's plate. "Some of the families around us have lost their land because of heirs' property. They fought as hard as they could but some of them just couldn't afford legal help, or they had distant relatives come in and ruin everything."

"I can't believe this. First Little Dove's pregnancy, now this. I deserved to know. I'm still apart of this family."

Mama Maggie tried to console Sparrow. "Well, you're here now baby. I'll show you everything they've given me. What type of law you practice anyway?"

"Personal injury. I can find someone to consult on our case though; that won't be a problem. What's his name?"

"Amos Jennings of Los Angeles, California. Handsome man, smooth talking; don't trust him though. He ain't no better than the ones they sent before."

"Did he leave a card? Have you signed anything? Please tell me you haven't signed anything."

"You think your grandmother stupid eh? I may not be college educated like you but I know better than to sign something before I talk to someone about it."

"I'm not calling you stupid Mama Maggie. I just want to make sure they aren't taking advantage of you. Corporations and their attorneys' prey on people your age."

"Where you think you get them smarts from? Me. Here's his card." Mama Maggie slid the business card across the table to Sparrow.

The ancestors listened in on the conversation below. Moon and Sibby were relieved that Sparrow was finally clued into everything going on within the family. Stepney was finally calm again, ceasing the rain. Moon's faith in Sparrow had been reignited so she shared her thoughts.

"I think hearing about the land sparked a fire in Sparrow. Maybe this will be the motivation she needs to embrace the family again."

Stepney was skeptical. "I don't know, Moon. Sparrow has disappointed us all, time and time again. This time may be no different."

Thunder commented. "She doesn't specialize in the type of help the family needs anyway, so what's the point?"

Arrow was astonished at what he was hearing. "We mustn't be negative. She said she can find the help we need, and we have to give her a chance to do so."

Sibby chuckled at Arrow's optimism. "Let's not pretend like you've always been a fan of Sparrow. She has made a lot of questionable decisions. But to be fair, I agree, we should give her a chance to redeem herself; if fighting for the land reignites her passion for this family then so be it."

The ancestors listened in on the rest of the conversation while August, Mama Maggie, and Sparrow talked. A shift in the atmosphere could be felt by the ancestors as Sparrow laid out a plan for the family's defense against Amos Jennings and Sunset Corp. She spoke with passion and intent. For once, it seemed as if she truly cared about what happened to someone besides herself. For the sake of the family, the ancestors prayed she didn't let them down.

August gave Sparrow a ride back to her hotel in Charleston. They hugged one another tightly before they parted ways. Sparrow took her time going to her room. She had no clue what type of mood David would be in. She stopped by the bar to get a drink first. She gulped down the dirty martini and made her way upstairs. She entered the room just as David got out of the shower. They greeted one another with a hug and kiss although there was still some tension between them.

Sparrow took a shower while David ordered room service. Once the food arrived, they sat at the table and ate quietly for a moment. David spoke first.

"I want to apologize to you about earlier. I spoke out of turn."

"I should apologize as well. I haven't been one hundred percent with you. I promise to do better about that moving forward."

"I appreciate that. I love you and I just want to be a part of your life and that means all of you."

"I love hearing that. How was your day?"

"I literally woke up maybe an hour and a half before you got back. Despite the argument with Gentry, I did have a good time last night up until that point. Duck and Gentry showed me a damn good time."

"I'm glad you had a good time." She paused. "I have some news."

"You talked to Gentry?"

"No, I haven't seen him yet. I didn't think it was a good idea to approach him so soon. But I swear to you, he and I will have a conversation."

"Ok, I'll take your word for it. You have to stand firm on what it is you want; I know you only want the best for the baby. What news do you have?"

Sparrow sighed. She could feel her stomach turning again. "A company called Sunset Corp has been sending attorneys at Mama Maggie's neck trying to buy our land."

"Really? What do they want to do with it?"

"Resort development. We have twenty-five acres of land. There are surrounding families too. Some have already lost their land due to heirs' property."

"I bet they are offering a pretty penny."

Sparrow was appalled. "David! That land is the mere essence of what it is to be a Singleton; it doesn't matter how much they are offering. She shouldn't let it go."

"I hear you but imagine what your family could do with that money; for starters, they could franchise the restaurant. You're the one always saying your folks need to move towards the future."

Sparrow paused before speaking. The thought of franchising the restaurant never occurred to her; maybe that was the future she so often talked about. "You make a good point. I never thought about that."

"You and your family should definitely look into it. The food is amazing, and the clientele is loyal. They could reimagine that all over the state, just to start."

"I would have to convince Mama Maggie and Uncle Elijah though."

"Why them?"

"Mama Maggie is our matriarch and Uncle Elijah is the oldest son. Nothing happens in this family without their approval. If they are on board, everyone else follows suit."

"You should draw up a plan and present it to them then."

"I haven't done a business plan since undergrad. That would have been more up Little Dove's alley. She was the business major."

"Stop doubting yourself; you're more than capable."

"Thank you for believing in me."

"Always."

David and Sparrow made love that night; a way to show their forgiveness of one another. They spent the rest of the night pillow talking about their future and what it would look like with GirlChild in it. Sparrow was scared to tell David about her greatest fear; her plan being rejected by her family. She wanted her plans to be successful although she knew they were radical. Isata made it clear they weren't going to let GirlChild go anywhere, but David had convinced Sparrow that she was invincible; and no one could tell her no. Sparrow just hoped it would all work out.

Chapter 14

"Ola, Isaac, she's lost her damn mind I tell ya! I can't believe she raised her voice at me." Isata vented to her husband and sister-in-law over a cup of coffee when they got home from work that evening. Gentry could hear the commotion and emerged from the bedroom and joined them. Isata told them about the disagreement she and Sparrow had. Gentry shed some light on what happened between him and David. Ola and Isaac couldn't believe their ears. Isaac had always been Sparrow's biggest advocate but this time she was out of line.

"I won't let her take GirlChild. Isata, Isaac, I love you and this family, but it'll be a cold day in hell before Sparrow takes my daughter away from me. She's all I have left of Little Dove." Isaac understood. "She's all we have left of Little Dove too. Don't worry son, GirlChild isn't going anywhere." Gentry nodded his head in appreciation of his in-law's support. He retreated to the bedroom to check on the baby.

Ola rubbed her sister-in-law's shoulders to relieve tension. Over the years, they had become best friends. From the day Isaac brought Isata home to meet the family, Ola and Isata clicked; they were truly sisters. Ola delivered Duck, Sparrow, and Little Dove. She even helped nurse Isata back to health during a miscarriage Isata suffered a year after Little Dove was born. Ola was the aunt that played a pivotal part in the upbringing of Isaac's children. She babysat them, she healed them, and she loved them like they were her own. Ola never had children of her own because she was so dedicated to taking care of her family. She still lived with Mama Maggie. "Sister, we gone get through this; don't let this defeat you."

Isaac tried to reassure his sister and wife. "I'll talk to her; I'll clear this up and set the record straight." He wasn't looking forward to having a disciplinary conversation with his daughter. For so long, he defended Sparrow because deep down, he once felt as she did. There was a point in time when he didn't see a future on the island. He thought he was destined to do more than tend to a rice field. He went to school to be an accountant. He wanted to leave South Carolina and start his own firm one day but after the passing of his father and the birth of the restaurant, he realized his family needed him. His family's needs were more important than his dreams or at least that's what he thought. Isaac always admired Sparrow's tenacity and determination. Of all of their children, he knew Sparrow would fly the highest.

It was time to reel Sparrow back in though. Isaac was in denial for years but hearing what Isata and Gentry said confirmed for him that he had been enabling Sparrow for far too long. He didn't know where he would start but he knew he couldn't put the conversation off for long. If Sparrow was going to spend the next couple of months home, she was going to have to get with the program and show some respect. Isaac just hoped she didn't feel backed into a corner, causing her to go back to New York and never return to South Carolina again. He couldn't lose another child. When Sparrow ran off to New York at eighteen, Isaac and Isata were devastated. Now that she was back home, they didn't want to lose her again.

The following morning, David prepared to leave for New York. They made love early that morning, knowing they wouldn't see one another for a few months. They checked out of the hotel and took a cab to the bus station where they said their goodbyes. David reaffirmed Sparrow. "Don't forget what I said, you are strong. You have to put your foot down with your family. See this through." He hugged her and kissed her on the forehead before getting onto the bus.

Sparrow caught a cab to a local café to have breakfast. It felt good to finally be alone with her thoughts. She ordered a cup of coffee, scrambled eggs, toast, and bacon. She pulled a notebook out of her bag and began taking some notes. She wanted to gather her ideas for the family restaurant and draw up a concrete plan.

As she ate and made notes, she thought about how much drama had occurred since she got back home. *Should I just go back home?* David's words echoed in her head, *see this through.* She realized she had grown apart from her family and that she was more forward thinking than ever before, but she hoped it wasn't too late to bring them into the light. She needed them to see the future they could have.

She finished off her breakfast and coffee. The server came over and removed the dishes from the table. Sparrow paid for her food and left a tip. She got up and walked toward the restroom to go use the payphone. She needed to call a cab to take her over the bridge to get home. As she walked down the narrow hallway toward the restroom, she bumped into a woman and Sparrow's bag fell out of her hand onto the floor. They both bent down at the same time to pick up the items that spilled out and when their eyes met, Sparrow realized it was her high school classmate and old neighbor, Mahogany.

"Sparrow Singleton, is that you? Oh my God, it is!"

"Mahogany Templeton? Girl, it's been ages."

"I know! I'm in town visiting my family. I live in Alexandria, Virginia now. What are you doing here?"

Sparrow's head dropped. She hadn't said the words to anyone yet. "My sister passed. I'm in town for a while getting some things together."

Mahogany's hands flew up to her mouth. "Little Dove? Are you serious? I'm so sorry for your loss." She embraced Sparrow briefly.

"I'm still processing. It's so fresh. She had a baby and died from some postpartum complications."

"I truly hate to hear that; I know how close you two were."

"She was my beam of light."

Mahogany could sense Sparrow was taking Little Dove's death hard, so she changed the subject. "I planned to stop by Singleton's Kitchen before I leave town. I wanted my husband to have some authentic Gullah food."

"You're married? Never thought I'd see the day independent Mahogany settled down."

They both laughed. "Every strong woman needs a strong man. What about you?"

"I'm based in New York. My boyfriend and I live in Manhattan."

"Really? Nice."

"I was just about to call a cab to take me over the bridge. My boyfriend left two hours ago to return to New York on the bus."

"A cab? Girl I'm going that way now, you can just ride with me."

"You sure you don't mind? I don't want to interrupt your plans."

"I don't mind at all. Let's get out of here."

Sparrow and Mahogany caught up during the ride over the bridge. Mahogany's family had the neighboring land next to the Singletons. They had about fifteen acres. Sparrow and Mahogany had been classmates from elementary to high school and always got along. Mahogany was bullied as well for speaking Gullah when they were students at the academy on the mainland. She and Sparrow always talked about how they would get away from the island and make a name for themselves. Mahogany was now a nurse practitioner.

It occurred to Sparrow that the Templeton family may be dealing with the same issue as her family. She didn't want to pry but she needed to know. She decided to ask Mahogany a few questions anyway. "If you don't mind me asking, has your family been approached by Sunset Corp?"

"Girl yes! Yours?"

"I just found out they've been talking to my Mama Maggie when everyone else is at work."

"Those bastards; I'm told they've been sniffing around for the past year or so trying to buy as much land as they can."

"Mama Maggie told me some families have lost their land due to heirs' property."

"That's true. You remember the Archie family? They didn't have a deed to the land and a relative of theirs from Chicago came down and caused pure hell. The cousin wanted to sell. They lost everything."

"Wow. That's crazy. Does your family have an attorney yet?"

"My parents and grandparents say we don't need one right now. We have the deed. They can make all the offers they want. We're not going to sell. The land has been in our family since after emancipation. I don't have to tell you though; you know the history."

"You don't ever think you guys should just take the money and invest in the future?"

"Girl no; our land is the future, otherwise they wouldn't want it."

"Good point."

Mahogany dropped Sparrow off and promised to see her again before she returned to Virginia. Sparrow thanked her for the ride and information about Sunset Corp. Sparrow walked up the driveway and thanked the ancestors that Isaac and Isata's vehicles weren't there. Her intention was to speak to Gentry alone with no interference. After speaking with him, she would walk across the way to go sit down with Mama Maggie and Uncle Elijah.

When Sparrow walked into the house, she could hear Gentry in the kitchen. She entered the kitchen and saw that he was holding GirlChild in one hand and fixing a bottle with the other hand. "Good morning Gentry, you need some help?" He ignored her and continued fixing the bottle and rocking the baby. Sparrow sat down at the kitchen table. "We need to talk. Please let me explain." Gentry looked annoyed but he sat down at the table and began feeding the baby.

"Explain."

"I owe you an apology. The things David said were out of context. My intent was to have a conversation with you when I felt you were ready to receive what I had to say. I know you're overwhelmed with the loss of Little Dove and taking care of a newborn."

Gentry said nothing so Sparrow continued.

"I wanted to propose to you that you and I take turns with GirlChild until she was of age to go to school. I figured she could spend seventy five percent of the time here and summers with me to start. I did discuss with David that going to school in New York would be a good investment in her future, but I never said I wanted to take her away from you."

"Why do you think you know what's best for my daughter? There are good schools here too. If it weren't for the schools here, you wouldn't be who you are today."

"I just want her to have the best. The best also means…" Sparrow hesitated to continue, knowing she was going to strike a nerve.

"What? Say it."

"It means considering changing her name. How is she going to get a decent job? What about when she goes to school and kids make fun of her? I know what that feels like."

Gentry stood to leave. He was fuming. "How dare you! There is nothing wrong with her name. It was what Little Dove wanted. I loved your sister with every fiber of my being; I plan to honor her wishes in the upbringing of our daughter. If you loved Little Dove, you would get on board."

Sparrow lashed out. "Don't you ever question my love for my sister. Little Dove was my sister before she was ever your wife."

"And there it is, that sense of entitlement. You think the world revolves around you but it doesn't. You hate yourself and you have for some time now. I don't want GirlChild to grow up with animosity toward her family in her heart."

Sparrow stood up; now she was pissed. "How dare you!"

Gentry was done; there was nothing else to be said. It was apparent they weren't going to come to an agreement. He ignored Sparrow and walked down the hall and back into the bedroom, slamming the door behind him.

Sparrow sat back down and slammed her fist into the table. What had she just done? The situation worsened in a matter of minutes because she didn't know how to control her mouth. How could she get Gentry to see that she only wanted the best for GirlChild? Sparrow reevaluated her line of thinking and she still didn't think a name change was outrageous. Who would really hire someone named GirlChild Parish? She wanted to march into the bedroom and yell at Gentry and make him see reason, but she knew it was a lost cause for the day. She would revisit it at another time. She needed to go talk to Mama Maggie and her Uncle Elijah before he went over the bridge for the day.

When Sparrow walked into Mama Maggie's, she was welcomed by laughter. Elijah and Mama Maggie were at the dining room table talking and laughing over a cup of coffee. Sparrow kissed Mama Maggie on the cheek and hugged Elijah before joining them at the table. There were biscuits and jam in the middle of the table. Sparrow grabbed a saucer and fixed up a biscuit.

Sparrow listened to her grandmother and uncle talk about how well the restaurant was doing. They also gossiped about some of the regular customers. Sparrow finished off two biscuits and went into the kitchen to wash her plate. When she returned to the table, Elijah announced he had about thirty minutes before he needed to leave to go over the bridge.

"What you need to talk to me and your grandmother about, Bird."

"Well, for starters, I saw Mahogany this morning. She gave me a ride here."

"The Templeton girl? That was nice of her; I remember when she was yay high."

"Yep, Mahogany Templeton."

Mama Maggie chimed in. "The Templetons are good people; always been grateful to have them as neighbors."

"Well, about that; I figured since the Sunset Corp approached you, they must be approaching neighboring landowners. Mahogany told me they've made an offer to her grandparents too. "

Mama Maggie provided some insight. "I know. I talk to Ellen Templeton all the time. They offered them a pretty penny too when they first approached them."

"Mahogany says they aren't going to sell."

Elijah agreed. "I don't blame them. Our people worked too hard for this land to just up and sell it to those greedy bastards because they want to build yet another resort."

Sparrow realized Elijah would be tough to crack. He was obviously on the same page as the rest of the family. His thoughts toward Sunset Corp caused a decline in Sparrow's confidence on presenting her plan. David's words rang in her head again; *see this through.* She decided to test the waters anyway.

"Well, have ya'll weighed the pros and cons of selling?"

Elijah was taken aback. "What pros could there possibly be other than uprooting our way of life and starting over?"

Mama Maggie stayed silent. She wanted to hear what Sparrow had to say.

"There are pros and cons to every situation. What if we sold the land and took that money and franchised the restaurant? That would be an outstanding legacy to leave behind."

A hearty laugh released from the pit of Elijah's belly. He couldn't believe his ears. "Bird, you been in New York too long. This here a family business, we don't mind being local. We have an edge no other restaurant does and that's why we do so well."

"But imagine multiplying that ten times over and opening Singleton's Kitchens all over the state. And that's just to start; it could be a national chain one day."

Elijah went from laughing to a tone of seriousness. "Bird, I'm going to stop you there. We aren't selling."

Mama Maggie said nothing. She didn't come to Sparrow's defense or offer her thoughts on the matter. It was obvious in her silence that she stood with Elijah. Sparrow felt defeated and embarrassed. Elijah got up from the table and kissed her and Mama Maggie on the cheek before leaving for town. Once they were alone, Sparrow confronted her grandmother.

"Why didn't you say anything?"

"There was nothing to say. Elijah is the head of this family now and I trust his guidance. In what world do you think we'd give up this land?"

Sparrow didn't respond. It was like talking to a brick wall when talking to any of her family members. They refused to see that there was so much more out there in the world for them. Mama Maggie and Elijah were stuck in their ways. Sparrow knew if she couldn't get them on board, none of the family would follow.

Mama Maggie could see that Sparrow wasn't happy with her refusal. She knew getting through to Sparrow would be tough, but she didn't think it would be this hard. Mama Maggie wasn't prepared to give up so easily though. Sparrow had always been a stubborn child growing up; once she had her mind set on something, there was no changing it. Mama Maggie prayed that the ancestors and God would help Sparrow see reason.

Sparrow got up from the table and hugged Mama Maggie. "I'll see you later, okay?" Mama Maggie nodded her head. "I'll be here." Sparrow grabbed a napkin and biscuit to go. She wanted to lay down. She suddenly had a headache. She wished David was still there and by her side. She walked home across the way and went to her bedroom to nap. She just hoped that when she woke up, she would be in a better mood.

Chapter 15

As Sparrow slept, she felt a chill over her body. She began panicking and felt as though she couldn't breathe. She tossed and turned but couldn't shake the feeling. "It's okay sis, I'm here. I got you." Sparrow couldn't believe it. It was Little Dove.

"What? How is this happening right now?"

"You manifested my presence. I miss you so much."

Sparrow began to cry. "I miss you too, Dovey. Why did you leave me?"

"I didn't know this would happen. I'm so sorry."

"I don't know how I'm going to do life without you. Everything has been so hard lately."

"But you're strong, you're going to get through this."

"I pissed Gentry off so bad. He hates me."

"I'm sure he doesn't."

"I only want what's best for GirlChild. I want her to have a good life."

"Who says we didn't have a good life?"

"We did but things could have been better."

Sparrow reached out to Little Dove but couldn't get her within her grasp. She just wanted to hug and hold her sister again. Little Dove began to dissipate, and Sparrow started to panic. She called out for her sister over and over again until she was gone. "Sparrow, baby, wake up." Isaac nudged Sparrow repeatedly. She was talking in her sleep and her face was wet from tears. He worried a hag may have been present. Sparrow finally woke up and lunged into her father's arms. "I saw her!"

Isaac was confused. "Saw who? A hag?"

"No, I saw Little Dove. It felt so real."

"I understand. You miss her. We all do."

"No Daddy, this felt so real; she said I manifested her presence."

"I believe you, baby."

Isaac held his daughter and let her cry it out. She hadn't needed him in forever, so he savored the moment. He decided not to have that talk with her right of way after all and to revisit at another time. She had been through enough.

Stepney was disappointed in Isaac. He couldn't believe he wasn't going to confront Sparrow about her recent actions. Stepney believed that to spare the rod was to spoil the child. Isaac always ran to Sparrow's rescue when she was younger, and it was time he started calling her out. Arrow and Thunder agreed with Stepney; Sparrow had been a headache for far too long. Sibby and Moon disagreed; they both had a soft spot for all of the children. Even though Sparrow was a troublemaker, she still needed someone in her corner. Isaac was that someone. If Sparrow was to be held accountable, it had to be done from a place of love and who could do that better than Isaac.

Thunder expressed his concerns. "If Isaac puts that talk off for too long, he won't be able to get through to her. She'll just keep stirring up trouble."

Moon came to Isaac and Sparrow's defense. "Let us not forget why Isaac is always defending Sparrow."

Sibby nodded her head in agreement. "Isaac used to be Sparrow; remember when he wanted to leave the island and be a big man on his own?"

Moon continued, "He thought the island would be his downfall. If it weren't for old man Singleton's death, there's no telling if Isaac would have ever returned home."

Arrow joined in. "I remember now. You're right. He sees himself in her and that's why he gives her so much grace. I understand but that doesn't mean it's right."

Thunder changed the subject. "We are missing the bigger picture. She saw Little Dove. What if Little Dove can guide her from beyond the grave? What if Little Dove can get her to see reason?"

Stepney agreed. "Sparrow and Little Dove had a very special bond. If anyone can get Sparrow to see reason, it would be Little Dove."

The ancestors discussed the future of the family. God often told Stepney and Sibby how Sparrow would be the family's saving grace. Stepney and Sibby reiterated this to the rest of the ancestors and in turn, the family believed the same. Everyone was counting on Sparrow but her latest actions made Stepney and Sibby question God; something they rarely did. Would Sparrow be able to meet God's expectations?

The next morning, Sparrow woke up early. She went into the kitchen to phone David before he got up for work. He answered on the first ring. They expressed how much they missed one another. David was tired from the bus ride and hadn't gotten much sleep since he got in a little after midnight, but he decided he was still going to go to work.

"I'm going to go into the office around noon so I can sleep in a bit and then I'll leave the office around six or seven."

"Good; I know you're tired. I can't believe you're even going in."

"You have to work hard to be partner babe. I need to show my face."

"I know, I know."

"How did everything go yesterday?"

Sparrow sighed out of frustration. "Do we have to talk about it?"

"I think we should."

"Yesterday was so emotionally taxing for me. Everything went the opposite of how I wanted it to go."

"Start at the beginning."

"I met with Mama Maggie and Uncle Elijah. He all but laughed in my face when I suggested they consider the pros and cons of selling the land."

"Did you mention the franchise potential of the restaurant?"

"I did and he all but told me to kiss his ass! He said we aren't selling the land. If I can't get him on board, no one will hear what I have to say."

"Your family is so backwards. I've never heard of anyone turning down that much money for some swamp land."

"I don't get it. We could do so much with that money."

"How did your talk with Gentry go?"

Sparrow tried to hold back tears; thinking about how she offended Gentry almost brought her to tears. It made her think of Little Dove. "It was horrible. He went off on me. He's not going to let me bring GirlChild to New York and he damn sure isn't going to change her name."

"I thought him to be a more reasonable man. How is he going to raise her alone? He isn't thinking about her future."

"I agree. He's just emotional because of Little Dove's passing and I get it, but he needs to see the bigger picture."

They talked for thirty more minutes before Sparrow ended the call. She could hear her parents rummaging around in their room. She wasn't ready to face Isata yet. She tip toed down the hall and just as she was about to enter her bedroom, Gentry opened the bedroom door. Sparrow stopped dead in her tracks. To Sparrow's surprise, he asked her to watch GirlChild while he got ready. He needed to go to work for a few hours to handle some things. Sparrow was elated; she knew he was still upset with her, but this was a step in the right direction.

Sparrow took GirlChild into her arms and returned to the kitchen to fix a bottle. She didn't know how Gentry did it. It took her almost twenty minutes to fix a bottle with her free hand. GirlChild was such a good baby; she didn't even cry while waiting for her bottle. Once Sparrow had the bottle ready, she gently placed it to GirlChild's mouth, and she happily accepted. Sparrow returned to her room to avoid her parents. She would see them later when they returned from the restaurant.

After GirlChild finished her bottle, Sparrow burped her and laid her down on the bed. She lay next to the baby and stared at the ceiling. "I don't know what I'm doing here. Your mama should be here with us. I never thought I'd see the day when she wasn't here with me." Sparrow looked over at the baby. "You're a good listener. You can't fuss back at me like the adults do." GirlChild cooed at her aunt. Sparrow talked and GirlChild had no choice but to listen until they both dozed off to sleep.

Sparrow woke from her nap to the smell of chicken frying. The baby was still asleep. Sparrow placed GirlChild in her arms and took her across the hall and put her in the bassinet. She figured Gentry was home. She went into the kitchen and to her surprise, it was Isaac. He was cooking lunch.

Sparrow greeted her father. "Hey Daddy, you're not working today?"

"Took the day off. You hungry?"

"Yea, I'm starving."

"GirlChild still asleep?"

"Yep, I put her in the bassinet."

"She'll probably need a bottle soon. She won't be sleep for much longer."

"I'll fix it."

Sparrow got out the formula and a clean bottle and started to mix the formula. Isaac rarely took off work. She was curious as to why he was home in the middle of the day.

"What are you doing home? Is everything okay?"

Isaac chuckled. "Everything is fine. I just wanted to spend some time with you; especially after last night."

Sparrow hung her head in shame. "Oh, that. It was definitely an out of body experience."

"Let's talk." Isaac turned the burner on the stove off and wiped his hands on a dish towel. He sat at the kitchen table and motioned for Sparrow to join him.

"Let me start by saying that I love you, Bird. I'm so glad that you're home. I know I've been busy with the restaurant and rice field, but I really am happy that you're finally back."

"I love you too, Daddy."

"Now, it has come to my attention that you have been butting heads with certain family members. I want you to know that I come from a place of love, and I have no intentions of arguing with you. You are an adult as am I; we can talk things out."

"I agree."

"I wanna tell you a story about the time I almost left the island."

Sparrow was shocked. "What?"

"Can you believe it? There was a time when I hated it here. When you grow up in a big family like mine, it's hard for parents to invest in everyone's individual dreams. Elijah was the oldest son and king of the castle second to Daddy. It was assumed we would follow in Elijah's footsteps and that my sisters would follow in Mama's footsteps. I didn't wanna be no farmer. All of my sister's didn't want to stay home barefoot and pregnant. In high school, I shied away from speaking so much Gullah. I wanted to speak a 'proper tongue.' Going away to college was the best thing to ever happen to me; it showed me a new world. I was active on campus and met people from many different walks of life. When I finally settled on my major, I realized the possibilities were endless for me. But when I met your mother, she made me see that it was important for me to be my whole self every day and that meant not being ashamed of who I was. She showed me by being herself and encouraging me daily. When we graduated, we were still living in Columbia, saving money to move to Washington, D.C. because it was up and coming for black people. When your grandfather died, there was no question in Isata's mind that we needed to move to the island because family came first, but I hesitated. I questioned myself. What would become of my dreams? I came back home, and Isata helped me see that I can realize my dreams anywhere. I fell in love with home again and I vowed to never turn my back on this place or my family."

Sparrow thought about what Isaac said and spent a few seconds gathering her thoughts before speaking. "I had no clue you used to feel that way. Why are you just now telling me this?"

"I never wanted to influence you when you were younger. All of your decisions should be your own. We have raised you to be an independent woman. Little Dove took on a more nurturing role and had dreams of starting a family, but you have always been industrious."

"I really didn't come home to start drama. I just want what's best for everyone. I think I've always felt like a black sheep of sorts, and it makes me feel like I'm always in defense mode."

"Well now you know, your Daddy was a black sheep too, but I found a way to blend and stand out at the same time. You have to find your balance."

"Thank you for talking to me and not talking at me. I appreciate that."

"Of course, my Bird. Now, you know you owe some people an apology don't you?"

Sparrow sighed but she took accountability. "Yea, I do."

Isaac hugged Sparrow and returned back to the stove to finish cooking. Sparrow finished making the bottle just as she heard the baby crying. Gentry walked in the door just as Isaac was plating food. Sparrow returned to the kitchen with the baby and joined Isaac and Gentry at the table. They talked and ate; Sparrow even apologized to Gentry in front of Isaac and Gentry agreed to put it behind them. Sparrow just hoped Duck and Isata were as forgiving as Gentry.

Chapter 16

Later that night, Sparrow borrowed Isaac's truck to go into Charleston. Duck agreed to have dinner with her at a steakhouse called, *Chopped.* The talk with Isaac had given Sparrow the courage to apologize. When she arrived, she gave the host her name and was led to a table near the bar of the dimly lit dining area. She ordered a gin and tonic until Duck arrived. She was nervous but she knew it was something she needed to do. Duck arrived five minutes later, and the host brought him to the table. He ordered a drink and Sparrow ordered an appetizer of crab cakes.

Duck observed his surroundings. He had to admit, the place was nice, but he didn't want to seem impressed. He wasn't ready to give in to Sparrow just yet.

"So this is where all the muckety mucks have dinner and close business deals."

Sparrow chuckled. She knew he was holding back. "I guess so. I've never been here but I hear it's the best in town."

"You dine at places like this often?"

"Back in New York? Yes, we wine and dine a lot."

Duck sucked his teeth and rolled his eyes. "So, what did you want to talk to me about?"

"Can we order dinner first? The appetizer hasn't even made it to the table yet."

"I'd prefer to know what it is I'm walking into first; that way I'll know if I even need to order dinner."

Sparrow threw up her hands. "If you insist; I brought you hear to discuss our last encounter. Things didn't end on the right note, and I want to apologize for the things I said."

"You insulted everything we are."

"I know I did and I'm sorry; that's not what I meant. I spoke out of frustration."

"You've always spoken your mind, Sparrow but the things you said were downright awful. Is that buckra putting things in your head?"

"David has only supported me the best way he knows how; he isn't putting things in my head. I think and speak for myself."

Sparrow paused to think about what she just said. David was her support system. He understood her and her forward way of thinking. Although franchising the restaurant was his idea, he hadn't been a negative influence on her, or had he? Duck could sense she was second guessing herself. Sparrow ignored the doubt in her mind and continued.

"I just wanted to clear the air between us. I'm on an apology tour of sorts. I never meant to offend you or the family."

Duck took a sip of his drink. "Well, I accept your apology, but I don't know what you're going to do about Mama. She's pretty upset with you."

"She told you about our conversation?"

Duck laughed. "Of course she did, I'm her favorite child."

Duck's banter made Sparrow feel like a weight had been lifted off her shoulder. "You know what, I won't even debate that with you right now. I'm sure I'm no one's favorite at the moment."

The server returned to the table with two crabcakes. Duck ordered a medium well filet and Sparrow ordered a medium ribeye with a blue cheese crust. They ordered another round of drinks and talked about what was going on in their professional and personal lives. The conversation felt light but fulfilling to Sparrow; the way it should be. As they were finishing up their meal, a man walked toward their table and introduced himself. It was Amos Jennings of Sunset Corp. He extended his hand to Duck and then Sparrow.

"You're the grandchildren of Maggie Singleton."

Sparrow spoke before Duck could. "Yes, we are. You're the attorney from Sunset Corp, right?"

"Yes, Amos Jennings."

Duck joked. "They call you the devil around here."

Amos laughed. "I am offering temptation. Ms. Singleton, it's my understanding you practice law in New York."

"I do. Personal injury though."

"Ahh, I understand. Maybe you and I can talk over lunch, say tomorrow?" He offered her his card.

Sparrow looked over the card like she'd never seen it before. She paused for dramatic effect. She didn't want him to think she was eager to meet. "I think that would be a good idea. We can talk about why Sunset Corp has been preying on my grandmother."

Amos laughed once more. "You pick the place and time and I'll be there." Amos nodded his head to Duck and shook Sparrow's hand one more time before departing.

Duck was intrigued by the exchange. "Were you just flirting or was that lawyer talk?"

Sparrow blushed. "Both. Now let's get out of here."

When Sparrow got back home, she made sure Isata and Isaac were in their bedroom. She was still avoiding her mother until they could have a one-on-one. She went into the kitchen to give David a call. He answered on the third ring.

"Hello?"

"Hey baby, it's me."

"Ah, hey babe. I dozed off for a moment. Work was crazy today."

"I bet. Have you eaten?"

"Yes, I have. Chinese. What about you?"

"I met Duck at a steakhouse for dinner. It was pretty good."

"A steak sounds good."

"We had crab cakes too."

"I bet they were fresh and delicious."

"They were."

There was silence on the line for a few moments. Sparrow couldn't tell if he was just tired or uninterested. Or was she distracted and still thinking about her encounter with Amos Jennings?

David yawned on the other end. "Tell me about your day."

"Well, for starters, I had a talk with Daddy. He shared some personal information with me that made me rethink the way I've been approaching everyone lately. Gentry and I made up. I even watched GirlChild some today."

"Oh, that's great. So has Gentry changed his mind about anything you said?"

"He hasn't, but you know what, that's okay. He has community here and if he chooses to raise his daughter here, then that's his choice. If he chooses not to change her name, I have to understand that; supporting him means supporting Little Dove."

David scoffed. "I can understand not compromising on letting her come to New York but not changing her name? That's ridiculous. It doesn't make sense. How would he know what your sister wanted when she's not here?"

Sparrow couldn't believe her ears. "What did you just say?"

"I didn't mean it like that; I just meant he can't know if Little Dove would have compromised or not, she's not here to say so. He moved himself from Mississippi to South Carolina for a better life himself; he has to understand what that's like."

David struck a nerve, and he didn't even realize it. Sparrow snapped before *she* realized it. "How dare you? Your job as my partner is to support me and my choices. You have overextended yourself and your opinion of my family and I don't appreciate it!"

Before David could respond, they were interrupted by a slow clap. Sparrow turned around and it was Isata. She had been eavesdropping. Sparrow ended the call quickly and put the phone back on the receiver. She was embarrassed. She wasn't ready to talk to Isata but now was the time whether she liked it or not.

Sparrow motioned for Isata to sit down. Isata sat down and folded her arms. She was ready to give Sparrow an earful.

"Mama, were you eavesdropping?"

"Of course not, I come to the kitchen to get some tea. I only heard the tail end of the conversation."

"And?"

"And I'm glad you put that damn buckra in his place!"

"Stop calling him that; he's not a bad person."

Isata frowned. "He has a nasty spirit; speaking on a family he knows nothing about."

"He doesn't have a nasty spirit, Mama. I should have set a boundary; I should have educated him."

"I'm glad you understand your part in this."

"I didn't at first, but Duck made me realize it's my place to enlighten David on our way of life. I hadn't done that, and I made him think it was okay to make suggestions about things he shouldn't have had an opinion on to begin with."

Isata folded her arms. "Hmph."

Sparrow reached over and touched her mother's hand. Her touch made Isata bring her defenses down and she unfolded her arms. "I owe you an apology, Mama. I never meant to disrespect you. I love you. I only want what's best for this family. But now I see that I was going about it the wrong way."

Isata shed a single tear. She held back from bawling. It was rare that Sparrow was soft and vulnerable with her, and she appreciated the apology. "I love you too, baby. Let's put this behind us."

Isata and Sparrow hugged. Sparrow brought her mother up to date about her day with the baby and Gentry's forgiveness. She also told her about dinner with Duck and running into Amos Jennings. Isata could sense there was some romantic interest there, but she didn't want to bring it up until Sparrow was ready. They talked late into the night before heading to bed.

The following day, there was a knock at Sparrow's door. Gentry asked her to watch and feed GirlChild while he showered and got dressed. Sparrow obliged; she enjoyed every moment she got to spend with her niece. She took the baby out of Gentry's arms and walked into the kitchen where she was greeted by Isata cooking breakfast. Isata wanted to make sure Sparrow and Gentry were fed before she and Isaac left for work. Sparrow began fixing a bottle while Isata fixed a plate for her.

Isata grabbed the baby to allow Sparrow time to eat. Issac joined them to have some coffee with eggs and bacon. Once Sparrow was done, Isata returned the baby to Sparrow and she and Isaac were out the door. Sparrow burped GirlChild and talked to her like always.

Even though GirlChild wouldn't understand a word her aunt was saying, Sparrow thought it was important to speak positivity over her niece.

Gentry came into the kitchen once he was dressed and fixed himself a plate. He loved how Isaac and Isata made sure there was always a meal around. He was thinking about selling the house on the mainland to temporarily move in with Isaac and Isata until GirlChild was old enough for elementary school. He wasn't sure how he would be able to raise a baby without them. They had been instrumental with getting up with him in the middle of the night when GirlChild was inconsolable and crying her lungs out. Ola was also a great help. He definitely had some decisions to make.

When Gentry finished eating, he washed the few dishes in the sink. He thanked Sparrow for watching the baby and announced he'd be going across the way to sit with Mama Maggie and Ola so they could see the baby. Sparrow waited until she heard the front door close to retrieve her purse from her room. She returned to the kitchen and rummaged through her purse until she found what she was looking for; Amos Jennings' business card. She dialed his cell phone number, and he answered after a few rings.

"Amos Jennings here, how can I help you?"

"Good morning, it's Sparrow Singleton."

"Ahh, Ms. Singleton! Good Morning. I take it you picked a place and time for lunch?"

"I have. Do you mind meeting me at Shuckers at one in Charleston?"

"I don't mind at all, see you then."

"See you then."

Sparrow got dressed for the day. She walked across the way to ask Gentry if she could borrow his truck for a few hours. Mama Maggie and Ola wanted to know where she was going but she wasn't ready to spill the beans. She had no clue what she was doing. She just offered that she was going to run some errands and stop by the restaurant. She spent a couple of hours at Mama Maggie's before walking back home to grab her purse and keys to head to Charleston.

Chapter 17

Coincidentally, Sparrow and Amos pulled up to *Shuckers* at the same time. They walked in together and were greeted by the host. Amos suggested they sit on the patio since it was a nice day out and Sparrow agreed. They both ordered daiquiris and fried crab claws as an appetizer. Sparrow couldn't help but observe while Amos ordered that his skin was glistening in the sun. He was a beautiful man and he carried himself very well. She was obviously attracted to him, but she had to focus on the issue at hand.

"So, Mr. Jennings …"

Amos interrupted. "Call me Amos, please. I insist."

Sparrow continued. "Amos. Can you tell me why Sunset Corp has been sending attorneys to meet with my grandmother alone?"

"You're an attorney. You already know the answer to that; why would we want outside influences in the ears of people we are making offers to?"

Sparrow smirked. "Touché."

"But to be clear, I've met with your Uncle Elijah as well. I'm the fourth attorney down from Sunset Corp. The others were white men who couldn't get the job done. Between you and me, they thought sending someone like me would be an appropriate touch."

"Oh is that so?"

"You see, my mother's family was from James Island. She got out of here the first chance she got and moved across the country to California where she met my father. They settled in Los Angeles before they had me and my siblings. Although I didn't grow up here, I have ties to South Carolina."

"Ah, I see. How long will you be here?"

"The Sunset Corp is giving me as long as it takes although my personal timeline is shorter."

"Ready to go home already?"

"Don't get me wrong, the sea islands are a lovely place. But I have established a life in Los Angeles where I have friends and family, I don't want to be away too long."

Sparrow raised her brow. "A family?"

"Just my parents, siblings, and a host of nieces, nephews, and cousins."

"I can understand wanting to return. I miss New York. The hustle and bustle of the big city. It's nice to slow down every once and a while and come to the South but I don't see myself making a life here again."

"You sound like my mother. She loves her South Carolina roots, but she said she wanted more out of life."

"Exactly; that's why I left."

Amos pivoted the conversation. "So why not convince your family to take the deal?"

Sparrow leaned in. "What is the deal exactly? I'm just curious."

Amos pulled a business card out of his pocket, flipped it over, and wrote a number on it. He slid it across the table. Sparrow picked up the card and her eyes bulged out of her head. She tried to compose herself quickly, but it was too late. She had revealed her hand to him and Amos released a hearty laugh.

"Nice, right? Sunset Corp isn't playing around. They really want to develop the island. They really want this land."

Sparrow tried not to trip over her words. It was a big number. "I won't lie, I think the offer is reasonable, but I came here to tell you that my family isn't selling."

Sparrow slid the card back across the table and Amos put it back into his jacket pocket. The server returned with their daiquiris and crab claws. Before digging in, Amos bowed his head, closed his eyes and prayed. Sparrow watched on in awe. *He's a praying man too?* She took a sip of her drink. After seeing the offer, she knew she needed to speak with Mama Maggie and Uncle Elijah again. There was no way they could turn down that type of money without consulting with someone.

Amos understood that Sparrow was protecting the interests of her family, but he could also sense that she was a forward thinker and that the offer Sunset Corp made was appeasing. He wanted to know more about her so he could figure out a way to make this deal go through. He knew he could be charming and that's one of the reasons he was so successful at what he did. He planned to get close.

"I respect your decision. Of course, I'll have to hear it from your grandmother first."

"She hasn't told you no?"

"She told me she had to consult with her son and the family attorney."

Sparrow realized she was the family attorney. All this time, Mama Maggie had been waiting on her to come home. "Well, we haven't consulted with anyone yet and as I said, I practice in personal injury only but I'm 99% sure it's a no."

"Well, I didn't just want to meet with you to talk business."

"Is that so?"

"I'll be honest, I find you attractive. Your grandmother also talks about you a lot. I feel like I know you already."

Sparrow blushed. She couldn't remember the last time a man besides David had given her a compliment.

"I think you're handsome as well. What has my grandmother told you? I hope she didn't embarrass me."

"She told me about how you left home at eighteen and went off to college. She said you were top of your class before going to law school. She also says you're the most stubborn of all of her grandchildren."

"So, she basically tells you all my business?"

Amos laughed. "She talks about your cousins too, but she missed you so much she couldn't help but brag about you."

The server returned to the table to take their orders for entrees. Sparrow ordered fried oysters with fries and Amos ordered a fish sandwich with fries. They finished the crab claws and daiquiris before ordering another round. Although Amos was a stranger to her, Sparrow enjoyed his company. She was used to only being around family and desperately needed an adult conversation with someone that had a different perspective. After they finished their entrees, they agreed to meet again soon before parting ways.

Stepney was disgusted. "How dare she sit up with that devil; the man that tryna take the land." Moon was surprised Sparrow was being so gullible. "I can't believe she willing to trade in a white devil for a black one." Sibby ignored them; she was tired of talking about Sparrow. The child caused more hell than the devil himself and Sibby was worn out. "Don't make nothing of it, the man is using her, it's clear."

The ancestors were growing tired; just when they thought Sparrow was turning around and coming to her senses, she goes and sits down with the enemy. Arrow suggested maybe Sparrow had a trick up her sleeve for Amos Jennings, but Thunder doubted the idea. Thunder suggested that Sparrow had only been with David in her young adult life. She hadn't really lived, nor had she dated a Black man since high school. Amos Jennings was a snake in the grass; in their minds, he was selling a dream.

Arrow understood where Thunder was coming from but pointed out that Sparrow was a smart young, woman and she would soon be able to see through Amos. Moon wasn't so sure. She pointed out that common sense and book sense were two different things. They were left at a standstill, back to square one, worrying about what trouble Sparrow would cause. It seemed like a never-ending cycle.

A few nights later, the Singleton family gathered at the restaurant for a meeting called by Sparrow. The restaurant was closed for the evening. All of Mama Maggie's children and grandchildren were present along with their spouses and of course, Gentry. They congregated and talked over a meal prepared by the aunts since it was dinner time. After they were done eating, Sparrow called the meeting to order. She asked August to take notes. Sparrow stood in front of her family, nervous as ever.

Mama Maggie and Elijah sat up front next to Isaac and Isata. Elijah looked annoyed and his stare made Sparrow even more nervous. Sparrow initially wanted to invite Amos to the meeting, but she decided against it. She knew it would piss off her family to have the enemy there in their personal space while they discussed such a serious matter. She cleared her throat and said a silent prayer before she began.

"Good evening family."

In unison, they sang out, "Good evening."

Sparrow continued. "I asked you all here today to discuss something that I was not privy to until I returned home. It was brought to my attention that for the past two years; Sunset Corp has been approaching Mama Maggie to sell the land for resort and retail development."

Sparrow looked out into the crowd and she could see faces turn from curious to irritated; but she continued. "I met with the attorney for Sunset Corp and he told me what the offer was; I thought it was a good idea that we have transparency across the board before Mama Maggie just tells them no."

Isaac's brother John stood up to interject. "I know that in hindsight, we share the land collectively, but the decision is Mama's, Bird. She get to decide what happens with it."

John's twin brother, James, stood up to add, "Mama and Elijah have always made good decisions when it come to this family. I see no need to question them now."

They both sat back down and returned the floor to Sparrow. "I'm not questioning them; I just want everyone to know what it is we're turning down. Mama Maggie is willing to consider everyone in this decision, aren't you?"

Sparrow put the spotlight on her grandmother. Mama Maggie eased out of her seat to stand. "I am willing to listen. I haven't made any promises." She sat back down.

Sparrow's cousin Sampson raised his hand. Sparrow pointed to him to speak. "So, what's the offer? I'm willing to hear it."

Sparrow paused for dramatic effect. "$350,000."

The room broke out into an uproar. Some were excited about what they heard, and others were disappointed one would even consider sale of the land. The room was split. Elijah stood and yelled at everyone to be quiet. He joined Sparrow at the front of the dining room and spoke his piece.

"I know that number sound appeasing to some of ya'll. When I heard it, I was shocked myself. Mama and I don't make decisions lightly when we think about the future of this family. We have 25 acres of land that includes our rice field and our homes. OUR homes; homes we built with our own hands. The future of this family depend on that land. Selling it is out of the question."

Elijah went to Mama Maggie's side and helped her out of her seat. He walked her toward the kitchen and out the back door to Elijah's truck. Everyone could hear the truck door slam and the engine rev up. They were gone.

Sparrow looked to her parents for some type of support but Isaac and Isata both shrugged their shoulders. The chatter started back up as members of the family argued with others about what should be done. Sparrow was disappointed in the outcome of the meeting. She looked to August but she was no help either. It was like she was out in the water stranded on a life raft alone.

Sparrow dismissed everyone. She went into the kitchen to help Isata and Ola with the dishes. They washed dishes in silence. Sparrow was tired of talking. She wanted to call David or Amos, but she would wait until she got home. She needed to have a mature conversation with someone.

Chapter 18

When Sparrow got back home, Gentry was on the porch with GirlChild. She joined him and they talked for a while. She watched in admiration as he spoke life and repeated positive affirmations to his baby girl. Sparrow knew Little Dove would have been so proud of her husband for the way he was adjusting to fatherhood. Sparrow underestimated Gentry but he was doing so well with the baby.

A warm breeze blew through the porch. Sparrow could smell rain coming. She inhaled the familiar scent. In New York, all she could smell was food and garbage; at home, the air smelled so clean and sweet. Gentry could smell it too. "You smell that? Rain coming." The baby begun to fuss. It was time for a bottle. Gentry took her into the house to get a bottle ready; leaving Sparrow to her thoughts.

The wind began to stir. The wind chimes rang out. Sparrow stepped off the porch and let her arms out to receive what was coming. The elements and nature always helped her connect to her emotions. She wished Little Dove was there. She felt like running away again but that wouldn't solve her problems. Her mind was all over the place.

It began to sprinkle. Sparrow called out toward the sky. "God, what am I doing wrong? Help me. I need you. I just wish my sister were here. I want my sister." It began to rain harder. Sparrow fell to her knees and cried. Isata ran out into the yard and held her daughter. She rocked her for a moment then brought her into the house. Sparrow sat at the kitchen table dripping wet while Isata fixed some tea to warm them both up. "Baby, you okay?" Sparrow didn't say a word, she just stared into the abyss.

Sparrow didn't touch her tea. Isata tried not to worry and told Sparrow she would give her some alone time. Isata retired to her bedroom. Sparrow waited until she heard her mother's door close to tip toe down the hall to her own bedroom. She changed out of her wet clothes and dried off before getting into some pajamas. Her hair curled up from the rain. She plaited it up and put on a scarf.

She got into bed and stared at the ceiling. Life had been turned upside down for her; how was she to go on living like this? Her sister was gone, and half of her family hated her at the moment. She wasn't talking to David either. She considered returning to New York once more but what would that solve? Sparrow rolled over to her side to get in a more comfortable position. She just wanted to turn her thoughts off and go to sleep but her mind was racing. She started to cry again before she eventually fell to sleep, praying Little Dove would appear to her once more.

Sibby and Moon watched from a cloud above. For once, they were able to observe Sparrow without the men hovering over them. Stepney never cared for Sparrow or her antics and Arrow and Thunder just agreed with whatever Stepney said. Sibby and Moon had both been mothers in their former life; despite her shortcomings, Sparrow was still a child in their eyes and children made mistakes. Sibby took it upon herself to invest in guiding the Singleton women in motherhood, so she too understood that children were not perfect and that the love between mother and child was unconditional.

Moon spoke. "That Sparrow is conflicted. She rarely pray."

Sibby agreed. "She taking Little Dove death hard. It's been blow after blow since she got here."

"I know you can't tell me, Sibby, but God will handle it, right?"

"Doesn't He always?"

"You're right. Stepney just make it seem like she a lost cause, but I know that's not true. She'll come around."

Sibby shook her head. "That Stepney, he be a hard one to please. His favorite be Little Dove and Duck; the non-problematic children. Stepney don't believe in a child causing a ruckus; that's why Sparrow such a hard pill for him to swallow."

"He don't like all the attention she's getting but he be the one tell us she going to save this family."

"He is still a messenger of God. He may not truly believe in the message but he not going to say so."

Sibby and Moon watched over Sparrow for a little longer; wondering if she would have a dream where she saw Little Dove again. Sparrow seemed to be sleeping peacefully. Sibby and Moon prayed together for Sparrow's healing and for the other ancestors to get on board. If they were in disarray, it would reflect in their guidance of the family. Sibby said a special prayer that God would soften Stepney's heart because she knew it would take him getting on board for Arrow and Thunder to follow suit.

Sparrow slept till about noon the next day. When she woke up, she didn't smell any food. She walked around the house, and everyone was gone. She took a bath and got dressed for the day. She didn't have any particular plans. She wanted to go into Charleston and find a coffee shop to relax and read. Gentry's truck was still in the driveway, so she figured he was at Mama Maggie's. She walked across the way and he was there with Mama Maggie and Ola. Mama Maggie was holding GirlChild.

Ola offered to fix Sparrow some lunch. Sparrow happily accepted. Ola went into the kitchen to fix her a plate. She sat at the dining room table across from Gentry. He was finishing up his plate. He leaned in and whispered to Sparrow, "You hear the news?"

"What news?"

"The Templetons lost their land."

Sparrow yelled out, "What?"

Gentry shushed her, he didn't want Mama Maggie to know he had spilled the beans. "Their grandmother called Mama Maggie this morning crying. You should call over to Mahogany."

He got up to take his plate into the kitchen. Sparrow called out to Ola and asked if she could get her plate to go. She also asked Gentry if she could borrow his truck for a few hours. Sparrow gave Mama Maggie and GirlChild a kiss before returning across the way. She wanted to call Mahogany right away, but she needed some privacy.

Sparrow recalled Mahogany's parents phone number like she was back in high school. A man picked up on the first ring. Sparrow announced herself and asked for Mahogany. The man called out to Mahogany to come to the phone.

"Hello?"

"Mahogany, it's Sparrow."

"Girl, I meant to call you this evening."

"What's going on?"

Mahogany burst into tears. "We lost it. We got backed into a corner and we're getting pennies for it."

"How did this happen?"

"My grandparents, they assumed they had a deed. Well, they never had a deed and can't find the will. Sunset Corp found out they had neither. We're going to lose everything. My greedy cousin, Hoyet, wanted to sell."

"Oh my God, I can't believe this."

"You better check with your grandmother, Sparrow. Get your affairs in order. Don't just take her word for it. Lay your eyes on the paperwork. I wish I did."

"Mahogany, I'm so sorry this happened. I need to make another phone call, I'll check on you later, okay?"

"Thank you for calling, Sparrow. I appreciate it."

Sparrow and Mahogany ended their call. Sparrow grabbed her purse and rummaged through it. She pulled out the business card she was looking for; she needed to call Amos. She dialed his cell phone number.

"Amos Jennings here, how can I help you?"

"Amos, it's Sparrow Singleton."

"Ah, Sparrow, how are you?"

Sparrow avoided the pleasantries. "Can you meet me in an hour and a half in Charleston?"

"Um, sure, where?"

"The Charleston Museum."

"Okay, see you soon."

Sparrow grabbed the keys to Gentry's truck and started on her way into Charleston. She didn't know what she was going to say or do but there had to be some way to help the Templeton family. She knew it wasn't her place, but she wouldn't feel right if she didn't try. When she got to the museum, she parked and waited in the lobby. She checked her watch after some time and noted that Amos was fifteen minutes late.

She purchased two tickets and grabbed some brochures to browse to pass the time. She sat on a bench near the door. A few minutes later, Amos rushed in. He apologized for his tardiness. Sparrow let it be known she was annoyed by her facial expression. They began the self-guided tour.

Amos was intrigued at the exhibitions. Sparrow thought it would be a good idea for him to see the history of what Sunset Corp was destroying. She eventually led him to the Lowcounty History Hall. They discussed Charleston's rich history. Although interested in what he was seeing, Amos was ready to cut to the chase.

"So why did you want me to meet you here?"

"I heard about the Templetons."

"Ah. The Templetons; I wanted to be able to hand them a better deal, but they didn't want to play ball."

"You don't feel an ounce of remorse, do you?"

"For what? Doing my job?"

"You're taking away their livelihood; do you know how long the Templetons have been on that land?"

"Key words: been on that land. All this time, they haven't thought to get their affairs in order? That's not my fault."

Sparrow grunted out of frustration. "Ugh, I can't believe you! You really are the devil."

"Sparrow, let's be realistic here, you know I'm only doing my job. Why does it even matter to you? This doesn't affect your family."

"You don't understand. Their loss is a loss for all of us. We are a community. Where do you expect them to go? What do you expect them to do?"

Amos threw his hands up. "Not my problem. At least your family has the restaurant to fall back on."

"What does that mean?"

Sparrow felt her heart racing and her stomach began doing back flips. Was Amos insinuating that her family was next? Was he trying to say they didn't have legal claim to their land either? Sparrow needed to speak to Mama Maggie and Elijah right away. She needed to know the facts. Sparrow didn't say another word, she left the exhibition and head back to the front of the museum. Amos followed in confusion.

"Where are you going?"

Sparrow fumbled with her purse until she found the keys to Gentry's truck. "I have some business to handle."

"You're leaving? We just got here."

"I'm sorry to have wasted your time."

Amos grabbed her hand. "You didn't. Can I see you again?"

Sparrow pulled away. "I don't know if that's a good idea, Amos."

"Don't let business interfere with what you think of me as a person."

"I'll call you. I have to go now."

Sparrow hopped into the truck and drove off, leaving Amos standing there in a trail of dust. She needed to speak to Mama Maggie, but she needed to stop by Elijah's office first. Elijah was a construction manager. He had been responsible for building some of the newer homes at Singleton Way. Sparrow pulled into the parking lot and got out. It was humid outside and she couldn't tell if she was suddenly burning up because she was frustrated or if it was the sun scorching the back of her neck.

Sparrow entered the office and was greeted by a receptionist. Sparrow introduced herself and asked for her Uncle Elijah. The receptionist buzzed into Elijah's office phone and announced Sparrow's arrival before showing her the way to the office. Elijah was shocked to see his niece; he immediately thought something was wrong or that there was a family emergency.

"What's wrong, Bird? What you doing here?"

Sparrow cut straight to the chase. "Does Mama Maggie have the deed to the land? Does she have a will?"

"What? Of course she does."

"Are you sure? Have you actually seen it?"

Elijah struggled to answer. "No, but why would she say she has it if she doesn't?"

"Did you know the Templetons lost their land?"

Elijah exclaimed, "What?"

"They assumed they had legal rights to the land. They didn't. It was heirs' property."

Elijah began pacing back and forth. Sparrow rubbed her temples. She needed to see Mama Maggie. The room began to spin; she needed some air. "I have to go. Can you call Mama Maggie and let her know I'm coming?"

"Sure. But what are you going to do?"

"I just want to make sure we're protected."

Sparrow turned to leave. She adopted a sense of urgency after speaking with Elijah. She was more worried than ever now. What if Amos and Sunset Corp were coming after her family next?

Chapter 19

Sparrow pulled into the driveway and went into the house. For some reason, she wanted to talk to David before she went to Mama Maggie's. Although they weren't on good terms, she did miss him and would potentially need his help. She called his office and got his voice mail. It was his lunch hour, and he was probably out with the partners. She paced the hallway waiting for the hour to pass.

After some time passed, Sparrow tried David again and got him. He sounded indifferent.

Sparrow tried to butter him up. "Hey baby, I miss you."

"What's going on?"

"I figured it was time we talk. I should apologize."

"You snapped at me. You've never snapped at me like that."

"I know and I'm sorry. I've just been so stressed lately."

"I get it babe, but we are adults; we have to be able to talk things out."

"I know, I know. It won't happen again, okay?"

David accepted her apology. His tone immediately changed from one of indifference to interest. "How are things going back home?"

"I don't even know where to start. Our neighbors lost their land to Sunset Corp."

“Wow, how did that happen?”

“It was heirs’ property. They’re getting pennies on the dollar for it now.”

“They should have taken the deal.”

Sparrow scoffed. “No, David, they should have been able to decide what they wanted to do with their land.”

“Sunset Corp is going to have their way one way or another. They are too big and powerful not to; they have resources that the families they are going after don’t have.”

“Well, that’s another reason I’m calling; I need a referral to a real estate attorney. I just need to consult someone on our options.”

David sighed. “Your family doesn’t have the deed to the land?”

“I honestly don’t know. I’m going to talk to Mama Maggie after I get off the phone with you.”

“I’ll get you Ashley Jones’ contact information; you remember her from school?”

“Oh yea, I remember Ashley.”

“Let me make some calls to see where she’s working now. Call me back tonight, I should have it by then.”

“Thank you so much.”

Although David offered to help her find a real estate attorney, Sparrow knew how he really felt. It was no secret he thought they should sell the land. He didn’t even entertain the idea that the Singleton family should weigh options. Sparrow now realized what Amos meant when he said the Singleton’s had the restaurant to fall back on; the Templeton family were everyday working people. Their land had been passed down throughout the years and they didn’t have businesses to fall back on. Sparrow thought about what would happen to them. It was too late for the Templetons, but she prayed it wasn’t too late for her family.

When Sparrow made it to Mama Maggie's, she could hear grandmother was upset with her; she usually offered food or tea at the very least, but she just pointed Sparrow to a chair. Ola joined them at the dining room table. She decided she would be a buffer if things got out of hand. Elijah phoned Mama Maggie ahead like Sparrow asked and he told her he had just learned the news of the Templeton family.

Mama Maggie got straight to the point. "Sparrow, explain yourself."

"Explain myself? Why didn't you tell me the Templeton's lost their land?"

"It wasn't my business to tell; nor was it Gentry's! And don't you be going up and down the island spreading the news. Let Elijah be the last person you tell."

"Mahogany was going to tell me anyway, Mama Maggie."

"Well, you should have waited until she called you. Can you imagine how embarrassed them folks must be?"

Sparrow hadn't even thought about it. She chastised herself in her head for doing what she always did; speaking before thinking. "I didn't think about that, you're right, I'm sorry."

"Now what you rush over here for?"

Sparrow decided she wasn't going to tell Mama Maggie about her outing with Amos. It would have just added more fuel to the fire. "I don't want what happened to the Templeton's to happen to us."

Mama Maggie sucked her teeth. "Since when you wanna keep the land; the one you run away from?"

"I just want it to be OUR decision whether or not we sell. I don't want anyone to bulldoze us into a corner."

"I don't know how to get this through your head, Bird. We ain't selling this land. Our people work hard to make it what it is today. Why would we throw that all away?"

"I get it now, I do. So help me, help us."

"Help you how?"

"Mahogany told me her grandparents didn't have a deed and they couldn't find the will. Please tell me you have one or the other or better yet, both."

"I'll be honest with you baby, you gotta prove to me you on the same page as the rest of us. How I know you won't go do what Hoyet did?"

Sparrow was insulted and concerned. She was insulted that Mama Maggie didn't trust her and she was concerned that referencing Hoyet Templeton meant that their land was in danger; did she not have the deed or a will after all? She took Mama Maggie's comment with a grain of salt. She needed to focus on the issue at hand. "Ola, can you step in here?"

Ola threw up her hands. She didn't want any parts of the back and forth. "Mama has a point, Sparrow. Ever since you got here, you been trying to convince all of us to sell. How we know you really understand the importance of the family legacy now?"

Sparrow realized Ola had a valid point. "I'll prove it to you, to everybody. I'm going to speak with a real estate attorney sometime tonight once David gets her number. I'll have some valuable information by morning."

Mama Maggie rolled her eyes. "I don't want that buckra in our family business. He ain't family. He don't care about what happen to our land while he lay up in a fancy apartment in New York City. What do you even see in him?"

Sparrow was ready for the conversation to end. "He's not family, yet. I just need his help on this one thing. It's not like he's going to tell anyone."

Mama Maggie repeated herself. "You heard what I said; family business is family business."

Mama Maggie got up and went to her bedroom. She didn't want to sit with Sparrow another second. Never had she ever gotten this upset with her granddaughter. Sparrow had always been wildly independent and hardheaded, but she never disrespected her grandmother. Ola saw no reason to sit around either. She went to sit out on the porch. Although she hadn't contributed much to the conversation, she agreed with Mama Maggie. Sparrow saw no reason to stick around at Mama Maggie's if neither she nor Ola were going to talk to her; she grabbed her things to go back home.

David called the house around six and provided Sparrow with their classmates' telephone number and email. Sparrow called immediately and left a voicemail on her house phone. Sparrow ate and played with GirlChild for a little while. She told Gentry about her talk with Mama Maggie. He apologized for even telling her the news. Mama Maggie chastised him when she found out he was the source. Gentry and Sparrow agreed it would be hard to keep the news from Isaac and Isata. They would find out soon but Mama Maggie's wrath was not worth spilling the beans.

Isaac and Isata were closing the restaurant for the night so they wouldn't be home for a while. Sparrow and Gentry sat out on the porch and just talked. A warm breeze swirled in between Sparrow and GirlChild's toes. The sun began to set. Finally, the phone rang, and Sparrow passed the baby to Gentry and darted into the kitchen.

"Singleton residence. This is Sparrow."

"Sparrow? Hi! It's Ashley Jones; I got your voice mail."

Sparrow let out of sigh of relief. "Ashley, thank you for calling me back, it's so good to hear your voice."

"No problem. How are you doing? David tells me you're in South Carolina for the summer."

"I am. My sister passed away unexpectedly so I'm here handling some business."

Ashley gasped. "I'm so sorry to hear that."

The line was silent for a moment. Sparrow hadn't meant to make it awkward, but this was her new reality; she was without her baby sister. "It's okay. Hey, I called because I need a consult."

"Sure, what's going on? David didn't really give me much detail; he just told me the venue."

"Well, my family lives on one of the sea islands of South Carolina; Huguenot to be exact. We have 25 acres of land. Most of the families around here have 10-50 acres of land; it varies. There's this developer, Sunset Corp, they're trying to buy up as much as they can for resorts and other retail."

"Ah, I see. So what is this, eminent domain, heirs' property, what are we dealing with?"

"There's a lot of heirs' property down here. One of our neighbors just lost their 15 acres and I want to make sure my family is protected, but this isn't my area of expertise and I need more information."

"No worries, girl, I got you. Get a pen and paper, you're going to want to take notes."

Sparrow placed Ashley on a brief hold to run to her room to get a notebook and pen. She ran back down the hallway into the kitchen to continue the conversation. "Okay, I'm back; give me the scoop."

Ashley spent the next hour giving Sparrow an earful. Sparrow couldn't write fast enough. "Hmm. Where do I start? Who is in charge of the family affairs?"

"My grandmother, Mama Maggie and her oldest son, Elijah."

"Okay, so you'll need to share this information with them specifically. Do you know who the land belongs to originally?"

"It's Singleton land, passed down to my late grandfather, to my knowledge."

"Okay good; so he would have left it to your grandmother?"

"Correct."

"Does she have the title and deed to the land?"

Sparrow hesitated. "I'll be honest with you. I don't know. When I first got here, I advocated for selling the land against their wishes. Things have changed since losing my sister and now I want it to stay in the family. My grandmother hasn't been very forthcoming with me about the specifics just yet because she doesn't trust me or believe in my change of heart."

"I understand. It's fine. We'll go over options then but when you regain her trust, it's important to nail down a title, deed or will."

Sparrow jotted down notes as fast as she could. "Understood."

"Do you have an understanding of what heirs' property is?"

"Can you enlighten me so I can verify if my line of thinking is correct?"

"Sure. Heirs' property is basically family land. It's usually been passed down to multiple family members after death without a will. Sometimes, there is a will. Either way, the multiple family members become tenants in common; the land isn't divided so they all own an interest in the land."

"Gotcha; that's helpful to know."

Ashley continued. "If your grandfather had a will, he would have died testate, meaning the will dictates who inherits the land. If he didn't have a will, he would have died intestate, and state law determines who inherits the land."

"Let's operate off the assumption there is a will."

"I'd rather prepare you for the possibility of either. You want to be smart about how you maneuver with companies like Sunset Corp."

"You're right; go on."

"Now, when the lane is inherited without a will, none of the heirs can claim a specific piece of land because they all have equal rights to the land. As tenants in common, any tenant can go to the court requesting a partition of the land."

"What happens then?"

"There is a partition in kind and a partition by sale; in kind means the land must be divided up equally. A partition by sale triggers a new process that requires the land be sold, usually to the public via auction."

Sparrow shuddered at the thought. Her family would hate her forever if they lost the land. She had to do something. "Oh my God. I feel sick. Ashley, if my family loses this land, it'll tear us apart."

"Trust me, I understand; I see this every day. Nothing tears families apart like death and the division of assets."

"Surprisingly, there was no fuss after my sister's death. Everyone loved her; she left behind her husband and a baby girl. There was no question everything would go to them. But the land is different; it's our legacy, our blood, sweat, and tears."

"I get it. I do. I applaud you for taking this step in reaching out. Your grandmother and uncle may be upset with you now but they're going to appreciate you later."

"Thank you for that."

"Now, where was I? Oh. We want to avoid a partition at all costs. Do you think any of your family members would go against the family's decision to sell if there is no deed or will?"

"Honestly, I think everyone believes I'm THAT family member. We had a meeting and I told everyone what the offer was for transparency, and it piqued the interest of some but the gavel was brought down by my grandmother and uncle. It wasn't pretty."

"Well, let's prove them wrong. Next, you need to make sure that the property taxes are up to date. Don't wait on a clear title or to verify if your grandmother has the deed, do that as soon as possible. The county tax assessors usually serve at least four notices of delinquency before the property is sold. Depending on the county, these things can be delayed. Every county tax assessor isn't caught up on these things, especially in smaller venues."

"I'll get right on that."

"Good. Give me some insight on how your family uses the land; do you all live on it, farm on it, or is it just sitting there?"

"Oh no, we have houses on the land, and we have a rice field. We sell the rice in our local restaurant and other stores in Charleston."

"Perfect. Then we don't have to go over adverse possession, condemnation, or eminent domain."

Sparrow was relieved that the conversation was over. Now she had an overwhelming amount of information to look into. She planned to go into downtown Charleston the following morning. She wanted to take heed to Ashley's advice and find what she could as soon as possible. Sparrow wanted to catch up in pace with Sunset Corp. She thanked Ashley for the consult; Ashley tried to reassure her and asked that Sparrow call back once she had more details.

Chapter 20

The following morning, Sparrow got up early and cooked breakfast for the house. Isaac and Isata were surprised by the gesture. Gentry joined them and they ate together before Isaac and Isata left for work. Once the coast was clear, Sparrow revealed to Gentry that she was on a mission, and she wanted him to join. Gentry hadn't really been getting out of the house lately besides going into the office occasionally to handle tasks his peers couldn't; plus he was the only one who knew what Sparrow was up to. She explained to him that she had a consult with a real estate attorney that gave her some homework. Gentry agreed for the ride along. They took turns getting ready so one could watch GirlChild while the other got dressed.

Gentry got Girlchild into her car seat and put her in the truck. Sparrow locked up and got into the passenger's seat. They crossed the bridge and drove into downtown Charleston. They pulled up to the county offices; their first stop was the county tax assessor. A young lady greeted them; she smiled when she saw GirlChild.

"How can I help you today?"

Sparrow stepped forward. "I'm trying to verify if the taxes on my family's property are paid, you know, if they are current."

"Sure, I can help you with that; what's the last name and property address?"

Sparrow provided the requested information and noticed a frown on the young lady's face. "What's wrong?"

"I'm not finding anything with that information. Can you verify the spelling of everything for me?"

Sparrow verified everything but the expression on the young lady's face didn't change. "Still nothing?"

"No, I'm sorry. You may want to verify what you have and come back."

"Okay, thanks anyway. Where can we go to see if there's a title and deed?"

"Go down that hallway and take a right then the elevator bank is on the left. The office is on the second floor."

"Thanks again."

Sparrow and Gentry took the elevator to the second floor to the Register Mesne Conveyance Office. They were greeted by an older lady who was enamored by how cute GirlChild was; she made baby sounds until GirlChild smiled.

"Such a beautiful baby. How can I help you all today?"

"We're trying to verify if a title is clear and if a deed is on file."

"Okay, what's the name and property address?"

Sparrow provided the information again with hopes of good news but once again, a disappointing look crossed the clerk's face. "Did you find anything?"

"I'm sorry, I didn't. I can double check though to be sure."

Sparrow spelled everything out again but still, there were no results. She and Gentry looked at one another dumb founded. They thanked the clerk for her time and went back downstairs and into the parking lot. They sat in the truck for a few minutes, lost about what they had just learned.

Gentry walked through his thoughts aloud. "Something is up; there's no way your family has a rice field and houses on that land and there's no title or deed? No record of property taxes? There's no way they've just been living on the land for ages."

"That's my reasoning too, Gentry. How could there be no records?"

"You need to confront Mama Maggie. There's something she's not telling you."

"I agree. I don't think right now is a good time to do that though. She's so upset with me."

"I get that, but you need to do it sooner rather than later. Sunset Corp isn't wasting any time so why should you?"

Gentry and Sparrow decided to surprise the family and eat lunch at Singleton's Kitchen. They invited Duck to drop by and join them. Sparrow knew Mama Maggie told her to stop running her mouth, but she figured she could confide in her big brother. They sat at a table in the kitchen. The restaurant was busy as usual, so no one would overhear their conversation. GirlChild was asleep in her car seat on the floor. Their cousin, June, took their orders and passed the ticket over to their Uncle Daniel to prepare their meals.

The food came out in no time. They dug in and ate in silence. Sparrow caught herself humming as she ate. Duck figured something was up when Gentry and Sparrow invited him to lunch. They had just been at odds and now they were all buddy, buddy. Duck confronted them.

"Why did ya'll invite me out? What's going on?"

Sparrow wiped her mouth before speaking. "Why does something have to be up for you to join us for lunch?"

"Really Bird? Be serious. You two were just at odds not too long ago."

Gentry laughed. "But we're good now; we're family, no need to hold grudges."

"Tell me what's going on or I'm calling Mama over." Duck leaned back in his seat like he was going to motion for Isata.

Sparrow grabbed Duck's arm and made him put his seat back down. "Chill out! We did bring you here to tell you something, but you have to swear to keep it to yourself."

"Okay, so spill it."

"The Templetons lost their land."

Duck was shocked. "What? How do you know that?"

"Gentry overheard Mama Maggie on the phone with their grandmother."

Gentry confirmed. "Yea bro, Sunset Corp got to them. They didn't have their paperwork in order."

"So why ya'll telling me this? What does this have to do with our family?"

Sparrow was suddenly quiet and poked at her food. She couldn't even form the words. Gentry stepped in. "It would appear, we don't have our paperwork together either."

Duck was confused. "What? How is that even possible? The land has been in our family for decades."

Gentry continued. "We went to the county office, and they can't even find the family land in the system under the Singleton name."

Duck shook his head and turned to Sparrow. "That can't be right; what are you doing about this? You're the attorney."

"Duck, I'm a personal injury attorney. This isn't my area of expertise. I did speak with an old classmate who specializes in real estate law but without Mama Maggie's cooperation, what can I do?"

"You can make her cooperate. Tell her she has to; we can't lose our land. Sunset Corp is going to eat us alive."

"No they won't; I'll make sure of it."

They finished their meals and Sparrow washed the dishes. They hung out around the restaurant for another hour or so before Duck left to run errands. GirlChild became fussy so Gentry suggested they return home so he could lay her down for a nap. Sparrow volunteered to drive so Gentry could soothe the baby on the ride over the bridge. She was ready to get home and have a private conversation with David.

When Gentry and Sparrow got home, Gentry went into the bedroom to lay down with GirlChild. Sparrow went into her parents' bedroom to grab the cordless phone. She went into her bedroom and sat in the middle of the bed with her notebook out. She called David at work and asked the secretary to transfer her to his line. After a few rings, David answered.

"David Roberts speaking."

"Hey, it's me babe."

"Hey, give me one second, let me finish typing the last few sentences of this brief so I can press send."

Sparrow waited a few minutes and could hear David typing on the other end. Once he was done, he returned to the line. "Okay, I'm done. How are you?"

"I'm as well as can be. I talked to Ashley last night."

"Really? What did she say?"

"She gave me a lot of information."

Sparrow went over her notes. It was a lot to digest as it wasn't something either of them specialized in. David took notes as he listened to Sparrow. Once she was done, he had questions.

"So, where does your family stand in the midst of this?"

"Unfortunately, Gentry and I took a trip downtown today and they can't find our records."

"Huh?"

"They can't find a record of the Singleton's occupying this land."

"That doesn't make sense; but a small island like that, the records could be mixed up somewhere or lost."

"I have no clue. I need to talk to Mama Maggie again though."

"Babe. I'll be honest with you. I think you should just come back home. You and Gentry have made up and the baby is fine. Let them deal with this headache. Why do you care so much? You don't even live there. Plus, if Sunset Corp figures out a way to make an underhanded deal, at least your family has the restaurant to fall back on."

Sparrow could feel her temperature rising. She was so tired of him inserting himself when it wasn't needed. She just wanted him to be there and listen. "Are you serious right now?"

"What? Your life is in New York now. You have me and a career; your future is here."

Sparrow was truly taken aback. There was no way David thought all she needed was him; yes, she had left home at an early age and hadn't returned in ten years, but she talked to her family on the phone every other day. The connection to family was still there. She couldn't believe he was suggesting she abandon them when she could be doing something to save them. David was just showing how truly selfish he was and that he didn't care about her after all. Although she promised she wouldn't lash out again, her temper got the best of her, and she released before she knew it.

"Let that be the last damn time you make a suggestion about what I do in regard to MY family; the people that love me most. You know what, throughout this entire process, from Little Dove's death until now, you have been an asshole. All you have done is made back handed comments about my family and our way of life. It makes me wonder what you really think of me!"

"I have been realistic from day one. You're coming from a place of emotion, and you aren't processing what I've been saying to you. Right now isn't a good time to do this, I'm at work for Christ's sake."

"Fuck you David! I'm done."

Sparrow hung up the phone. She felt a weight lift off her shoulders. David proved to be the devil her family thought he was; he didn't truly care. She didn't know what she was going to do when her time on the island was up. They had been together so long that she realized she depended on him far more than she needed to. She needed to free herself, so she did.

The family was going to be ecstatic to hear the news of Sparrow and David's break up. Sparrow would deliver the news over a meal. To cook, eat, and fellowship was the Singleton way. She returned the cordless phone to its cradle in her parents' bedroom before going into the kitchen. She looked in the fridge and freezer to see what was available to cook for dinner. Isata and Isaac usually kept the fridge and freezer stocked so there were plenty of options.

As she rummaged through the fridge, she realized she had everything she needed to make Frogmore stew. She would only need about thirty minutes to cook so she decided to take a nap until it was closer to dinner time. When she woke up, she pinched herself; had she really broken up with David? She giggled at the thought of finally being free from him and his repressive opinions. She realized she may be sad later once she dwelled in the breakup but for now, she was relieved. She went to the kitchen and began pulling out different ingredients.

Sparrow took out potatoes, ears of corn, shrimp, and smoked sausage links. She began to cut up everything except the shrimp. She husked and cleaned the corn and cut it into quarters. She decided to spice things up and add some blue crabs. She also decided on onions. She brought her seasoning and water to a boil in a large stock pot. She added the potatoes first, then the sausage and corn. The smell brought Gentry out of his room with the baby.

When Isaac and Isata walked thru the front door, they made a bee line into the kitchen. Sparrow was adding the shrimp and blue crabs.

Isaac was excited. "If you keep cooking, we may have to hold you hostage."

Sparrow smiled at her father. "You may not have to do that."

Isata was intrigued. "Why is that?"

Gentry couldn't contain himself and yelled out, "Sparrow dumped that buckra!"

Chapter 21

Isaac and Isata were astonished by the news, and they wanted answers right away. Sparrow instructed everyone to go into the dining room where she would serve dinner and they could talk. Sparrow elbowed Gentry before he left the kitchen. He just couldn't seem to hold water lately. Isaac and Isata quickly set the table. They sat across from one another giggling.

Sparrow brought the stock pot into the dining room and put it in the middle of the table. She fixed everyone's plate. Isaac said grace quicker than he ever had before giving Sparrow a piercing look. He wanted to know what was going on and he didn't want to wait another minute. He cleared his throat. "So? You have something you need to tell us."

"Yes, Daddy. I ended things with David today."

Isata shouted out, "Hallelujah!"

Gentry laughed so hard he snorted. "Told you they were gonna act a fool."

Isaac tried to hide his grin, but it was impossible. "I'm sorry to hear that? I can't tell if you're happy or sad."

"I haven't' decided just yet; right now, I feel free."

Isata rubbed Sparrow's back. "I'm so happy to hear that; now you can really soar, Bird."

Isaac had more questions. "What does this mean?"

"It means, I'll be here for a little longer than I originally thought."

Isaac fist pumped the air. "Yes! I never thought I'd see the day."

"I need to go back to New York at the end of the summer to get some more things. Do you mind coming with me?"

"Of course not, Bird. But we'll have to fly, my treat. I'm too old for that long bus ride."

Sparrow loved that sound of that. "Thank you, Daddy."

They dug into their Frogmore stew before it got cold. They spent the time at the table talking about how different things would be with Sparrow relocating back home. It felt good to hear how excited everyone was; she only wished Little Dove had been there to witness it. She couldn't wait to tell Mama Maggie; maybe it would soften her grandmother's heart and instill some trust back into their relationship. When they were done with dinner, Isaac and Gentry volunteered to clear the table and wash the dishes.

Isata and Sparrow sat out the on the porch with GirlChild while Isaac and Gentry cleaned up. They ate vanilla ice cream and warm pecan chewies for dessert. Isata rocked back and forth in the rocking chair and sang to GirlChild. She played with the baby's little toes. "I remember sitting in this same rocking chair with you and Little Dove ages ago. Ya'll were basically porch babies." Sparrow smiled at her mother. She was looking forward to being a porch baby again; in New York, there wasn't a 'porch' in sight. It was literally a concrete jungle.

Isata had something she needed to confront Sparrow about; although Sparrow was slowly coming around, she needed to know her daughter's true intent for returning to the island. She didn't want to ask in front of Isaac or Gentry; she needed to be able to look into her daughter's eyes and see the truth without anyone else in the room. "There's something I want to discuss with you."

"What's that Mama?"

"Why did you meet with Amos Jennings?"

"How do you know about that?"

"Girl I got eyes all over this island and in Charleston. Did you seriously think you would see him, and no one would know?"

"I didn't consider it. I forgot how small this place is; everybody is in everybody's business."

"Well, fess up, why have you been seeing him?"

"If you want to know the truth …."

Isata cut her off, "I do; that's all I want to know."

"I find him attractive. He's a very charming man. I also wanted to know what he had up his sleeve regarding Sunset Corp."

Isata studied Sparrow's face as she talked and concluded that she was being honest. "Thank you for telling me the truth. I think it's okay that you find him attractive but even snakes could be charming to others. Be careful with him."

"I will, Mama. There is no need to worry."

"I trust you'll follow your instincts."

Isata retired to her bedroom with GirlChild. She was going to give Gentry a break for the night. Isaac and Gentry transferred the basinet from Gentry's room into Isaac and Isata's room before kissing the baby and telling them goodnight. Gentry planned to go over the bridge to meet Duck at a bar. Sparrow decided to make one more phone call before she went to bed. She wanted to talk to Amos; she hoped it wasn't too late. She dialed his cell phone from memory this time.

"Amos Jennings speaking."

"Hi Amos, it's Sparrow. Did I wake you?"

Amos cleared his throat. He didn't want her to think he'd been asleep. "Of course not, I was just doing some light reading."

"Where are you staying?"

"The Francis Marion. Why do you ask?"

"They have a bar?"

"Of course; as a matter of fact, I think there's some live jazz going on down there tonight."

"I'll be there in an hour then. Meet me at the bar."

Sparrow hung up the phone before Amos could interject. She didn't know what had gotten into her, but she was feeling impulsive. She raced down the hall and went through her closet and threw on a dress. She removed her scarf and fluffed her curls; she studied her reflection the mirror. For the first time, she noticed Little Dove in the reflection. She whispered to herself, *you're always with me, Dovey.*

She threw on some complementing heels and strutted down the hallway. She was feeling herself and it was a good thing because she knew she would need the confidence boost. Isata poked her head out of her bedroom door. "Bird, I thought you were in for the night?" She turned on the hall light. "You look nice!"

"Thanks Mama, can I use your car for the night? I'm going over the bridge into Charleston."

"Sure, just be careful. Remember what I told you."

"I'll be careful."

Isata retreated back into her room. Sparrow grabbed the car keys and went on her way. An hour later, she was parked but not ready to go in yet. She asked herself aloud, "*What the hell am I doing?"* She got out of the car and walked through the lobby like it was her runway. She felt sexy and now she just wanted to be desired. As she approached the bar, she noticed Amos immediately. He sat at the bar with a glass in hand, grooving to the sounds of the live jazz band on the stage. There was an empty seat next to him.

With no warning, Sparrow sat down next to Amos. He was surprised she actually showed up. The bartender greeted her and took her order. She requested a martini, stirred, extra dirty with three olives. It was going to take liquid courage to get through the night. Sparrow turned her back to Amos to tune in to the band. He admired her from behind; she was indeed a sight to see. They didn't make women like her in Los Angeles.

The band finished their first set and announced they would be taking a brief intermission before they started back up. Sparrow turned her attention to her drink and sipped it slowly. Finally, she turned to Amos and acknowledged him by smiling at him. He could pick up what she was putting down; she was playing hard to get and he didn't mind chasing her one bit.

"Ms. Singleton, what brings you out this evening?"

Sparrow took another sip before she answered. "I felt like a night out on the town. I realize I haven't shown you the other side of Charleston yet."

"Is that so?"

"You've been so busy doing the devil's work, you haven't had time to enjoy his playground; the nightlife of Charleston."

"I'm listening."

"You're in for one hell of a night. You ready?"

Amos downed the rest of his whiskey. "I'm following your lead."

Sparrow finished her martini and paid the bartender for both of their drinks. Amos wasn't expecting her to cover the check. He would redeem himself later. Sparrow suggested he take his suit jacket back up to his room and meet her in front of the hotel while she brought the car around. He did as he was told and took his jacket back to his room; once there, he checked his breath and sprayed on extra cologne. He couldn't believe he was trying to impress a client beyond business means. He asked himself, *"Is she flirting or genuinely trying to convince me the land is worth leaving alone?"*

Above, Sibby and Moon watched Sparrow; observing her had become an emotional rollercoaster of sorts. Sibby and Moon went from excitement over the breakup with David to tears because the family sat down to dinner to enjoy the news of Sparrow returning home to confusion.

Moon blurted out, "what the hell is that girl doing, Sibby?"

"Don't ask me, I'm just as lost as you."

"She go from leaving that buckra to announcing she's staying home and now she out with that snake."

Sibby agreed. "She's being so impulsive. I don't understand it myself."

"I'm just glad Stepney, Arrow, and Thunder ain't here to see it."

"I agree."

Moon wasn't ready to leave yet. She was too invested in how the night was going to turn out. Sibby didn't want to leave either. They both hoped Sparrow knew what she was doing.

The first stop on their tour was to a hole in the wall called *Blood Hounds*. They found an empty table for two and ordered drinks. Sparrow drank Alize while Amos sipped on a White Russian. The sound of blues blasted all throughout. There was no way he would be able to have a conversation with her there; it was too loud. He yelled out, "It's kind of loud in here." Sparrow put her finger to his lips. She leaned in so he could hear her clearly. "We didn't come here to talk. We came here to dance."

She took down the rest of her drink before getting up and grabbing Amos. He followed her out onto the crowded dance floor. Sparrow began to groove to the music. Amos didn't know what to do, he wasn't much of a dancer. He was impressed by Sparrow's moves though. She grabbed his hands and guided them around her waist. He began to allow the music to enter his veins; in no time, they were in sync. They danced for about twenty minutes before returning to their table.

Amos broke a sweat and grabbed a napkin to wipe his forehead. Sparrow was amused. "You not used to dancing, I see." Amos was slightly embarrassed she noticed. "Not really, it's not my thing but I'm really enjoying myself."

"Good, because it's not over. Let's go."

Amos didn't ask any questions. He followed Sparrow back to the car and she drove to the next spot. The next stop was a juke joint called *Grasshoppers*. This spot was well known for its fried chicken plates and live music. They sat at the bar and ordered a couple of Smirnoffs. Sparrow recognized the bartender from high school, and they chatted for a bit before she ordered a fried chicken plate to share with Amos.

Sparrow asked Amos if he was rested enough to dance again. *Doo Wop* by Lauryn Hill came on and before Amos could answer, Sparrow was dragging him out onto the dance floor. "This is my jam!" She danced circles around him. Amos wasn't sure if it was the alcohol or not but the more she danced around him, the more he could see colors emitting from her aura; warm blues, reds, and oranges swirled around them. Amos began to rock back and forth to the beat. He pulled Sparrow into his body, and they grooved together. They were a sight to see out on the dance floor.

They danced for two more songs before they returned to the bar. Their fried chicken came out just as they sat down. It was hot and fresh out the grease. Sparrow inhaled the scent of the food. Amos reached in for the kill, but Sparrow popped his hand. She tore off a piece of the chicken thigh and fed him. Amos' eyes rolled into the back of his head as the flavors danced on his taste buds. Sparrow asked him, "Good, right?" Amos nodded his head in approval, grabbed a fork to taste the red rice and again, he gave a stamp of approval.

After they ate, Sparrow announced it was time to go. She would take him one more place before they retired for the night. Sparrow was a bit tipsy, but she was still cognizant. The last stop was at a lounge called *The Lake Lounge.* It was R&B night. Amos paid at the door for the both of them. Sparrow grabbed his hand and led him to the cigar bar. They ordered two cigars before finding a velvet couch near the DJ booth. A server stopped by their table to light their cigars and take their drink orders. Sparrow ordered a Tom Collins to start, and Amos asked for a whiskey sour.

They puffed on their cigars and enjoyed the sounds of the music bouncing off the walls. Amos commented on how good the DJ was; the DJ played Janet Jackson, Mary J. Blige, Mariah Carey, Erykah Badu, and En Vogue just to name a few. There weren't many lounges like this in Amos' neighborhood back home. Sparrow informed him it was black owned. Amos was impressed. He looked around and everyone was just vibing and talking.

By the end of the night, Sparrow was drunk. Amos carried her out of *The Lake Lounge* and lay her across the back seat of the car. He wasn't even embarrassed; he just saw it as a sign of a good time and a successful night. He drove back to his hotel and valeted the car. He carried Sparrow into the elevator and to the fifth floor where he was staying. Sparrow would wake periodically and apologize. Amos got her into the room and took off her shoes. He laid her in the queen sized bed and pulled up the covers. He was going to sleep on the couch. As he pulled up the covers, Sparrow woke for a second and planted a kiss on his lips before passing back out. Amos grinned; he knew she liked him. He turned off the lights, got on the couch, and was asleep in no time.

Chapter 22

The next morning, Sparrow woke up freezing. She was confused and in a daze. *Where the hell am I?* She looked around and realized she was in Amos' hotel room. She couldn't believe she had gotten drunk and had to spend the night. On the pillow next to hers was a note that read: *Thank you for a good time. Out trying to close a deal. Valet has the car. Hope to hear from you soon.* Sparrow balled the note up. There were so many questions, and her head was hurting too bad to even think straight. *What did we even do last night?*

She got up and turned the air down. She went into the bathroom and looked in the mirror. She looked so disheveled; her mascara was running, her lipstick was smeared, and her curls were flattened against her scalp. She used the hotel's soap and shampoo to freshen up. There was no way she was going to take the walk of shame in her current state. She ordered some room service to get some food on her stomach because she was feeling queasy but after she ate and vomited a few times, she felt like herself again.

Sparrow found her heels in front of the closet. She put them on and left the room. She walked thru the lobby like she belonged there and got Isata's car from valet. As she drove back home, she started to remember bits and pieces from the night before; she had been a different version of herself. She looked in the rearview mirror and smiled back at her reflection. *You naughty girl.*

As she pulled into the driveway, she noticed Isaac and Gentry's trucks were gone which meant she didn't have to face them and Isata right away for not coming home last night. She got out of the car and took off her heels. As she walked barefoot up the driveway, she could hear someone call out to her, "Come here gal!" She turned around and it was Mama Maggie yelling at the top of her lungs from across the way. Sparrow rolled her eyes; she was not ready to face Mama Maggie yet. She walked back down the driveway and crossed to her grandmother's.

Mama Maggie was sitting in a rocking chair on the porch working on a quilt. Sparrow joined her and sat in a rocking chair next to her grandmother. Mama Maggie lifted the quilt for Sparrow to see. "It's for GirlChild. I got pieces of Little Dove's favorite clothes in here." Sparrow smiled at the kind gesture. "It looks beautiful. I'm sure she'll cherish it once she's old enough to understand the importance of it."

"Mhm. So, looks like you been caught red handed. Isata ask me to sit out here to see you got home safely. Where you been?"

Sparrow made a note she would need to talk to some of her family members about how much they told her business to one another. "I had a night out on the town with a friend."

"A friend? Mahogany?"

"No, a male friend."

"That Amos Jennings, ain't it?"

"How did you know?"

"It ain't hard getting information out of Isata."

Sparrow sighed. "Yes, we went out but I just wanted to show him another side of Charleston."

Mama Maggie didn't look up from the quilt. "You like that man, don't you?"

Sparrow didn't say a word. She figured Isata had told all of her business already.

Mama Maggie continued. "He a handsome man. I just don't think it's a good idea to get personal with him. But, you grown, do as you please, just be careful."

"I will, Mama Maggie"

"What happened to David anyway?"

Again, Sparrow knew Mama Maggie already had the answers to the questions she was asking but Mama Maggie wanted to hear it from the horse's mouth. "I broke up with him."

Mama Maggie yelled, "Thank the ancestors! Thank you God!" She got up and did a praise dance and stomped her feet. "Does this mean you're coming home?"

Sparrow couldn't help but laugh. She didn't realize her family disliked David so much. "It just didn't make sense anymore ya know? And yes, I'm coming back home for a while."

"Oh honey it probably never made sense to begin with, but just because you leave that man don't mean you run up under another one."

"I know, I know. Amos is just different. I've never met a man like him before."

"Because you were blinded by that buckra."

"Okay Mama Maggie, I get it."

"Good. I hope you enjoyed yourself last night."

"I did, I think. I don't really remember much."

"You kids and that alcohol. It's the devil's juice. Gentry and Duck stumble in at the crack of dawn, singing all loud and waking up Isata, Isaac, and the baby."

Sparrow was tickled at the thought of Duck and Gentry having such a good time the night before. "Sounds like everyone had a good night but I tell you what, after last night, I won't have alcohol again for a while."

Mama Maggie gathered her things and suggested they go into the house because it was getting too hot for her. It felt good as they walked into the cool house. They sat in the living room and talked more. Sparrow thought it was a good time to talk about the land since Mama Maggie was in such good spirits.

"I need to talk to you about something."

"What is it?"

"Gentry and I went downtown and did some research. They couldn't find a record of our land under the Singleton name. Are we in trouble? Are we going to lose the land?"

Mama Maggie stopped to think.; her faith in Sparrow had only just been restored. Sparrow's breakup with David and decision to move back home were steps in the right direction but was she really ready? Mama Maggie decided it was time to stop holding out. "My name is Maggie May Gardner-Singleton; only child of Rufus and Lillie May Gardner. This ain't Singleton land, Bird, it's Gardner land."

Sparrow couldn't believe her ears. All this time, the land had been Gardner land and Mama Maggie never said anything. "Does anyone else know?"

"Nope, not even Elijah. You see, a woman's role is to uplift and support her husband and that's what I did. I allowed your grandfather to turn this land into an empire, but he was never satisfied; he always wanted more. He wanted the land in his name, but I wasn't going to just give my family's legacy away. Now that he's gone and all of my children and grandchildren have proven themselves, I know what to do."

"What does that mean?"

"It means the Singletons shall have their empire and legacy after all."

"Why are you just now saying something?"

"I couldn't trust you when you first got here, Bird. I mean, would you trust you? You weren't thinking about the family; you were thinking about yourself."

"I can understand that; I now realize my judgment was cloudy. Does Sunset Corp know the land is in your maiden name?"

"I don't think they do; they haven't mentioned it. But I tell you what, tomorrow morning, I want you to take me to get the process started, it's time to switch it over into the Singleton name."

Sparrow rubbed her grandmother's hand. She couldn't believe Mama Maggie finally let her guard down and trusted her with something so important. She felt relieved. The family land was going to be fine after all. She promised to keep Mama Maggie's secret. There was no need to go blabbing off about their personal affairs until the ink was dry and Mama Maggie was ready.

When Sparrow finally got home, she took a long, hot shower. She needed to wash the nights festivities from her skin. She felt dirty for some reason. She washed her hair as well to refresh her curls. When she was done, she got dressed and went to get the cordless phone. She returned to her room and dialed Amos' cell phone. He must have finally recognized the number because he answered on the first ring.

"Sparrow, how are you feeling?"

"Much better now that I've showered and gotten myself together."

"Good to hear it. I must say, you showed me a damn good time last night. I was wondering if we could grab dinner tonight?"

Sparrow wasn't so sure. "Before I answer, what happened last night?"

"Nothing, we had a good time. You kissed me and passed out; that's it."

Sparrow was embarrassed. She couldn't believe she kissed him. "I'm sorry about that."

"Don't be sorry; I'm not complaining. So, will you have dinner with me?"

"Uh, yea, sure. Where and what time?"

"Let's do Grant's at 7:30."

"I'll be there."

They ended the call after confirming their dinner plans. Sparrow decided she would nap; her head was still hurting a bit. She went to return the cordless phone to her parents' bedroom when she heard the front door open. It was Duck and Gentry. They both looked tired. She walked into the living room to speak.

"I heard ya'll got in at the crack of dawn."

Gentry smirked. "We did; my good brother showed me a crazy time last night."

Duck slapped Gentry across the back and laughed. "No, you showed me a good time."

Sparrow laughed at their bromance. "Where are ya'll coming from?"

Gentry sat down on the couch and began rubbing his temples. "From the restaurant. We tried to pick up GirlChild but Mama sent us home to lay down."

"Are ya'll still hungover? I have a headache too."

Duck plopped down on the loveseat. "Yep, we had a whiskey sponsored night. I need to lay down."

They all agreed it was time to lay down. Duck fell asleep on the loveseat. Sparrow and Gentry went to their rooms. Sparrow fell asleep in no time. She dreamed of her future, she dreamed of Little Dove; she thought about how proud her sister would be of her. Sparrow tried to manifest Little Dove again in her dreams, but she didn't even know how she had done it the first time. Whether she could see her sister again in this life or the next, she knew Little Dove was looking down on her, smiling.

Stepney held a council meeting. They met right before sunset. They sat on a single cloud. Moon looked over to the empty spot where Winter would have sat. She missed Winter and wondered if she got to live on through GirlChild or if she sacrificed her life to give GirlChild life; that much was never made clear.

Sibby and Moon agreed the night before not to tell the other ancestors about Sparrow's rendezvous with Amos Jennings. They would likely find out tonight on their own if the meeting wasn't dismissed before Sparrow left for her dinner date. Sibby nor Moon wanted to hear Stepney's rant. His emotions often started storms. Stepney called the meeting to order.

"I'm sure we are all aware of the news by now. Sparrow has broken up with her boyfriend and decided to return home on a more permanent basis."

Sibby added, "I think this a step in the right direction. Sparrow has finally turned herself around."

Moon agreed. "Being home has made her a different person; she's starting to love herself again."

Stepney continued. "Did any of you know this was Gardner land?"

Everyone shook their head and answered no. Stepney was shocked. "I didn't know either; all this time, I thought it was Singleton land."

Arrow questioned Stepney. "God didn't tell you? Why would He keep that from you and Sibby?"

Stepney answered to the best of his ability. "We are only privy to what He wants us to know when He wants us to know it. I guess we didn't need to know until now."

The men had a side conversation about the future of the land once it was in the Singleton name. If Mama Maggie thought her husband turned it into an empire, just wait until she saw what her children and grandchildren would do with it. Sibby and Moon sat on the edge of the cloud and spoke quietly.

Moon asked, "How do we get them off the cloud before Sparrow gets ready for her date?"

"I was thinking the same; I don't think they should know about her meetings with Amos just yet."

Moon agreed. "Stepney would be so furious it would rain for seven days and seven nights."

They both laughed at the thought. There were times Stepney had been so upset that it rained for weeks. Stepney eventually ended the meeting and they all parted ways. Moon and Sibby agreed to meet back at the cloud once the coast was clear. They wanted to watch over Sparrow for the night.

Chapter 23

When Sparrow woke up, she checked the clock. She had been sleep for most of the day. She checked the rest of the house and Duck was gone. Gentry was still knocked out. Isaac and Isata weren't home from the restaurant with GirlChild yet. She started getting dressed. Grants was fine dining and she wanted to look the part. She pinned her hair up and did her makeup.

Once she was dressed, she knocked on Gentry's door before entering. He was finally up but groggy. Sparrow let him know she would be going out for the evening. She suggested that he needed to shower before Isaac and Isata got home with the baby. Gentry agreed and got up right away. Sparrow still had Isata's car keys so she left a note on the kitchen table that she was taking the car to dinner and would be back later.

Sparrow crossed the bridge and drove into downtown Charleston. When she arrived, she could see what the hype was about; the building was grand from the outside. Sparrow valeted the car; and she was ready to see the inside. She walked inside and advised the hostess she was a party of two under the name of Amos Jennings. The hostess confirmed that Amos arrived and was awaiting her arrival.

As Sparrow followed the hostess to the table, she observed her surroundings. The restaurant was dimly lit. There was a grand piano being played at the front and a jazz singer serenading the crowd. Each table had a small lamp and unique flower arrangement. It was very intimate. Sparrow wondered why Amos chose this place out of all places. When they got to the table, Amos stood and walked around to pull out Sparrow's chair.

The server arrived soon after Sparrow was seated and asked for drink orders. Amos requested a bottle of their finest chardonnay, and he ordered a shellfish tower to start. Sparrow was impressed; he was such a take charge man. If she were back in New York, she'd be on the couch with David eating takeout and talking about work. Amos was a breath of fresh air, but she knew in the back of her mind that she needed to tread carefully.

A different server returned with a bottle of Chalk Hill and an ice bucket. The server poured a glass for Amos and Sparrow. Amos held his glass up and Sparrow followed suit.

"I'd like to make a toast."

Sparrow was still unsure about his intent for the night. "A toast to what?"

"To new friendships."

They clinked glasses before each taking a sip. Their server returned with bread and the shellfish tower. It was extravagant. The tower consisted of lobster, shrimp, oysters, and crab legs. They both dug in and sampled everything. Sparrow was impressed.

"This is delicious. How did you hear about this place?"

"I asked the manager at the hotel. He said it was the best around."

"He wasn't lying. It tastes so fresh."

Their server returned to take their order for their entrée. This time, Amos let Sparrow go first. She ordered scallops, crab fried rice, and asparagus. Amos ordered ahi tuna and broccolini. Amos poured them both another glass of chardonnay.

"I brought you here so we could have a conversation about the offer Sunset Corp has made to your family."

Sparrow put down her glass. "Is that so?"

"Yes; your grandmother trusts you and your judgment. I thought if I could appeal to you, you could appeal to her. I got the impression that you were open to the idea of selling the land."

Sparrow couldn't believe him. She was fuming on the inside, but she would play his game. "I remember what you said about us having the restaurant to fall back on; I mentioned it to David and he said we should take Sunset Corp's deal and franchise our restaurant."

"David?"

"My boyfriend; well, my ex-boyfriend."

Amos was relieved to hear that Sparrow was single. "He may not have been a good partner but he's certainly a great thinker; franchising the restaurant would be a wonderful opportunity for your family. You guys could double, even triple your worth and assets."

Sparrow smiled slyly. "I agree; I just don't know how to convince my family of that."

Amos leaned in like he was telling a secret. "What if I can get authority to sweeten the offer; maybe add a couple of more dollars onto it."

"Money talks, so they say. But between you and I, I haven't been able to find my grandfather's paperwork yet. Does that matter?"

"We can figure something out. I'm supposed to meet with your grandmother and uncle tomorrow morning at 10:30."

"Oh? They didn't mention it to me. I'll go over before you do to tell them about what we discussed."

"I would appreciate that; now, enough about business. Let's talk about how beautiful you look tonight."

Sparrow fought back the urge to frown and throw her glass of wine in his face. She was disgusted by him; did he think her stupid? He was using her; he wasn't truly interested. Sparrow couldn't reveal her hand though. She instead, decided to continue playing along. "Thank you; you don't look so bad yourself."

"Do you think you'll be up for another night on the town after dinner?"

Sparrow carefully declined. "I wish I could but I'm on baby duty with Gentry tonight. She has colic."

"Maybe another night then. I really enjoyed myself. I haven't had that much fun in a while."

A few minutes later, their entrees were brought out. They looked over everything before the server left the table. The food was delicious, but Sparrow no longer had an appetite. She didn't want to raise any suspicion so she ate what she could. By the end of the meal, she was so irritated that she lied and said she was full and couldn't manage to order dessert. The server boxed up their meals and Amos paid the check and left a hefty tip.

When they got outside, Amos asked that the valet bring Sparrow's car around first so he could see her off. He helped her into the car and leaned in to kiss her, but Sparrow turned her head and the kiss landed on her cheek. They said their goodbyes and Sparrow took off. Once she was out of sight, she burst into tears. How could she believe she had an organic connection with Amos? He was being the devil and snake that everyone called him; showing his true nature. He didn't care about cultivating a friendship with her, he just wanted to close a deal. Sparrow felt stupid but she gave herself a pep talk; that was the last time she would let Amos Jennings get the best of her. It was time to smarten up.

Sparrow woke up bright and early to meet with Mama Maggie and Elijah. She got dressed and walked across the way. Ola was heading out to go to the restaurant. Mama Maggie was cooking breakfast. Elijah was sitting at the dining room table sipping coffee and reading yesterday's newspaper that he brought home from work.

Sparrow greeted everyone before fixing a plate fresh off the stove. She placed it on the table in front of Elijah. Mama Maggie fixed a plate for herself, and Sparrow and Sparrow carried them into the dining room. They said grace before they ate. Mama Maggie was surprised when Sparrow chimed in during prayer.

Sparrow was eager to get some things off her chest. She talked in between bites. "So, I met with that snake last night."

Elijah was lost. "What snake?"

Mama Maggie answered. "The land man."

Elijah nodded in understanding as he ate his grits. "Oh, the devil."

Sparrow continued. "He told me he's coming over this morning to meet with you too."

Elijah checked his watch. "That's right; at 10:30."

"Well, he told me he's going to offer more money. He tried to convince me so I could convince you."

Mama Maggie chuckled. "What did you tell him?"

"I played his game. I told him I would suggest it. I want to see if he really offers a better number though; I gave him some bait and I want to see if he'll take it."

Mama Maggie welcomed Sparrow. "Stay for the show then, Bird."

Amos pulled up and parked in front of Mama Maggie's at 10:30 on the dot. Sparrow could hear his engine shut off. She looked through the blinds and watched him get his briefcase out of the car. Devil or not, he was still a handsome man. Sparrow jumped back from the blinds when he turned around so he wouldn't see her staring. He walked up to the door and knocked a few times. Elijah answered and welcomed him into the living room. Mama Maggie offered him a cup of coffee, but he declined.

Mama Maggie and Elijah both sat in chairs next to one another and Amos sat on the couch across from them. He laid his briefcase on the coffee table. Sparrow stood behind Mama Maggie and observed Amos; something about his energy was off.

Elijah started. "What brings you here today Mr. Jennings?"

Amos smiled like a Cheshire cat. "As you know, I have made quite an offer for your family's land on behalf on Sunset Corp."

Elijah confirmed. "An offer that we've turned down. I know you sent my niece over to convince us otherwise, but we haven't changed our minds. We aren't budging. Ain't that right, Mama?"

Mama Maggie rocked back and forth and rubbed her knees. "That's right, baby. We're not accepting the offer."

Amos opened his briefcase and handed Mama Maggie and Elijah both a piece of paper. Mama Maggie passed hers on to Sparrow while Elijah looked over his. "Well, I'm rescinding the offer."

Sparrow stayed calm; she didn't want her emotions to get the best of her. She had been blurring the lines of business and personal. "You're rescinding the offer?"

"A little birdie whispered in my ear so I did some additional research and couldn't find record of Singleton land. It's heirs' property and I have an August Singleton ready to make a deal."

Amos closed his briefcase and got up to leave. Elijah sat forward in his seat to say something, but Sparrow stopped him. "Let me walk Mr. Jennings out; I'll be right back."

Sparrow walked Amos to his car. She looked around to make sure no one was outside or within earshot. She stuck to the script and acted clueless. "Just what the fuck are you doing?"

"Woah woah, I'm just doing my job, Sparrow."

"You went behind my back after I told you something in confidence!"

"To be fair, I made it clear from day one what my intentions were; I am here on BUSINESS. All I did was conduct business."

"You really are the devil they say you are."

Amos sarcastically offered, "I really do hope we can get past this. I enjoy your company."

Sparrow yelled out, "Go to hell!" as she walked away.

Sparrow went back in the house where she was met by Mama Maggie and Elijah's confused faces. They wanted answers. Sparrow sat down and broke down what had just taken place.

"Last night at dinner, I baited Amos, and he took it. I told him I couldn't find my grandfather's paperwork for the land. I casually slipped in that when I told the family about the offer Sunset Corp made, August showed the most interest. I called August early this morning and roped her in and as sure as fat meat is greasy, Amos called her."

Elijah was impressed. "I always knew you would make us proud, Bird. I was lost for a moment there."

Mama Maggie walked over to Sparrow and kissed her on the forehead. "You did good, Bird. You did good."

Sparrow was angry at herself for ever getting close to Amos, but she was happy she was able to redeem herself with the family. She knew the war was just beginning but winning the first battle was a good sign.

Chapter 24

Amos was in good spirits as he drove back over the bridge to his hotel in downtown Charleston. He knew one way or another, he would get to the Singleton family. Sparrow was the key, and he finally knocked the door down. He did regret he wouldn't be able to maintain a relationship with her but that was the way of the business. His primary focus was achieving personal and business goals, not making new friends.

When he got back to the hotel, he grabbed a celebratory drink at the bar before going up to his room. He was in a damn good mood. He had been working on Maggie and Elijah Singleton for a year now. His hard work finally paid off. He went up to this room to call his boss and request some paperwork from the secretary.

He sat at the desk and placed a call. The secretary, Sheila, answered and recognized Amos' voice right away.

"Hey Amos, how is it going on the east coast?"

Amos was grinning so hard you could hear his excitement through the phone. "As a matter of fact, it's going great. Is the boss around?"

"That's good to hear. He's in, I'll transfer you."

Sheila transferred the line and Amos' boss, Derek Purdy answered. "Derek here."

"Hey, it's Amos. I have some good news."

"And I have some bad news."

Amos was confused. "I beg your pardon?"

"I received a call from an August Singleton today about some unsavory business practices on our part."

"What?"

"She claims you tried to seduce her cousin to get them to sell."

Amos was appalled. "I didn't try to seduce anyone! We had a few business meetings but that was it. They don't even have a clear title and deed to the land so why does this matter?"

"They do. Did you not read the file thoroughly?"

Amos stuttered. "I — ... huh? What? There's no record of the Singletons legally owning that land."

"Because it's not Singleton land; it's in their grandmother's maiden name. It's her family's land. Everything is accounted for and up to date."

Amos could not believe he had made such a rookie mistake. He was usually more thorough, but he had been banking on Maggie Singleton's incompetence and age. He let Sparrow bait him into thinking he was one step ahead. He couldn't be mad at anyone but himself. "What does this mean?"

"It means you're coming home. I'm putting Ellis Smith on it."

"Derek, let's not be rash, I can fix this!"

"You've had a year and you fumbled. Pack it up. I have a meeting. I'll see you next week."

Derek disconnected the call before Amos could respond. Amos slammed down the phone and paced the floor. He couldn't believe what just happened. How could he have missed such a pertinent detail? He punched the air and yelled out, "That bitch!"

The lunch hour at Singleton's Kitchen was busy as usual. Sparrow and August sat at a table in the kitchen, laughing over tea. They couldn't wait to see what would happen to Amos. No one else knew of their plan except Mama Maggie and Elijah. Sparrow felt relieved to finally be free of the all the devils in her life. She had been the victim of self-hate, David's repression, and Amos the snake.

"I can't believe we pulled this off. God is amazing."

August agreed. "You should have heard him when I told him I was willing to sell. You could hear him grinning through the phone, that bastard!"

"You should have seen his face when he rescinded the offer. He was such an asshole about it."

"I can only imagine. Do you think he knows yet?"

Sparrow shrugged her shoulders. "I'm sure he'll know by end of day. We'll see."

When the crowd died down, Isata joined the girls at the table. The restaurant was having *Family & Friends Day* in two days on Saturday. This was an annual event in which they invited the public and those in need to come enjoy lunch on them for free. It was a community picnic of sorts. August helped Isata plan and organize the event and it was always a hit. Isata informed Sparrow that she would be needed on Saturday to help serve. Isata opened her notebook and read off duties.

"Sparrow, I need you to help June, Lillie, and Isabella serve. You do plan on coming right? Well, you don't have much of a choice anyway."

Sparrow laughed. "I'll be there with bells and whistles on. Why didn't you ever tell me about this event? This is amazing."

Isata reached across the table and rubbed Sparrow's hand. "We started it after you left home. I was always so worried about how you were doing up there in New York that I often forget to tell you things. We have much to catch up on now that you're home."

Sparrow was touched. "Aww Mama, we have plenty of time to get caught up."

Isata continued. "August, I need you to make sure everyone gets a ticket so they can get a plate. I want you to do the new spotlight this year too."

"Whatever you need, Auntie."

Isata took down some notes before returning to the dining area. August and Sparrow continued their conversation.

August wondered if they should clue Isata in on what was going on. "Do you think we should tell her?"

"No way, Mama Maggie explicitly said to keep it between us."

"Okay, I won't say a word then."

Sparrow ate a late lunch at the restaurant and grabbed a to go plate for Mama Maggie and Gentry. She was sleepy and needed to take a nap. She drove back home and took a plate to Mama Maggie first. When she walked into Isaac and Isata's house, she kicked off her shoes by the door and went straight to the kitchen. Gentry was preparing a bottle.

"Thanks for bringing me a plate. Amos Jennings called you like three times already. I told him you weren't in. What's going on?"

Sparrow tried to hide the satisfaction on her face; Amos must have known they were on to him. She decided to keep her cool; Gentry couldn't hold water and she promised Mama Maggie and her Uncle Elijah that she wouldn't say a word. "Nothing, we had a disagreement; he's probably trying to suck up to me. I'm going to take a nap, if he calls back, tell him I'm still out."

Gentry knew something was going on, but he didn't want to push the subject. "Okay, I will."

Sparrow peaked in on GirlChild before going to her room. GirlChild was laying in the middle of the bed cooing. Sparrow picked her up and twirled the baby's gray patch of hair around her finger.

She couldn't help but tear up as she looked into GirlChild's eyes and saw a version of Little Dove staring back at her. She rocked the baby and kissed her before whispering to GirlChild, "this was all for you." Gentry entered the room with a bottle and Sparrow handed the baby over.

When Sparrow woke up, it was evening. She went out into the hallway and heard her parents talking in their bedroom. They were home early from work. Sparrow knocked on the door before entering.

"What are ya'll doing home so early? I thought ya'll were closing tonight."

Isaac answered. "Mama said she's cooking dinner tonight and she wanted us there. Your cousins are closing for us tonight."

Sparrow was curious if Mama Maggie was going to tell them about the land. "Am I invited? I'm hungry too."

Isata chuckled. "Of course, she told us to tell you too, but we didn't want to wake you yet."

"I'll get my shoes then."

Isaac stood to leave. "I'll let Gentry know to get the baby ready. You go ahead, we'll meet you over there."

Sparrow grabbed her shoes by the front door and put them on. She walked across the way when she noticed all of her aunts and uncles parked out front of Mama Maggie's house. Duck's truck was there too. She walked into the house without knocking and was greeted by the smell of food. She hugged her aunts and uncles one by one. Mama Maggie was a mother of eight, so she was used to cooking big meals. As Sparrow entered the kitchen, she noticed there was food every where. Ola and Lillie carried dishes out to the dining room table. Isaac, Isata, Gentry, and GirlChild arrived a few minutes later.

Mama Maggie asked that everyone crowd into the dining room so she could address them all at once. She prayed first before she began. No one knew the purpose of the spur of the moment meeting except Elijah; Sparrow had an inkling but wasn't sure. Mama Maggie sat down after the prayer. "I have something to tell the family. I'm getting up in age as you all know. I think it's time I pass a torch I've been holding on to for some time now." Mama Maggie looked at Elijah to continue.

"As you all know, Sunset Corp has been approaching Mama and I after the land for a while now."

The Singleton children looked at one another and nodded their heads in agreement and understanding. Mama Maggie picked back up, "I have a confession. There was a point and time in life where I was wildly independent like our young Sparrow. I didn't think I needed anyone to build the life I wanted until I met your father. Henry Singleton shared my dreams. As husband and wife, we built something special together as one. But … the land doesn't belong to the Singletons … yet."

There was chatter amongst the Singleton children and Duck. Everyone was confused. Mama Maggie raised her hand for them to quiet down so she could continue. "The land belongs to me. It was Gardner land; but thanks to Sparrow, it will be Singleton land by the end of next week."

Ola asked what everyone was thinking. "Mama, when were you going to tell us it wasn't ours?"

"When the time was right, and the time is now. You all have built a small empire of sorts and I'm very proud of what you have done and what the future holds. I wanted to make sure everyone, and I mean everyone, was ready to take this on."

Isaac raised his hand and asked, "you mean to tell me, you were waiting on Sparrow to come home to tell us? What if she never came home?"

Mama Maggie smirked. "I knew she would fly back home. I always knew. The land belongs to all of us; we all have ties to it but now that GirlChild is here, I think it's time we look to the future. The next generation has begun. The bickering we've done, the tears we've cried, none of it matters now. We focus on the future now."

Mama Maggie looked at the faces of her children and grandchildren. She was proud; everything had come together like she prayed, like God promised. Ola and Isata began fixing plates and they all sat between the dining room, kitchen, and living room. They ate and fellowshipped, their favorite pastime. Everyone eventually parted ways and went to their respective homes for the night. Sparrow stayed behind to help Ola and Isata cleanup for Mama Maggie. Ola and Isata cornered Sparrow once Mama Maggie was out of the kitchen.

Isata playfully interrogated Sparrow. "So you knew the whole time this wasn't Singleton land?"

"No Mama, I only just recently found out."

Ola joined in on the banter. "Why you ain't say nothing? You ain't been able to keep anything else to yourself, why this?"

Sparrow laughed. "Mama Maggie made me swear."

Isata and Ola were still shocked at Mama Maggie's news. Sparrow reassured them that the land was safe, and that the family didn't have to worry about anyone trying to sell to Sunset Corp. They finished cleaning up and Ola walked Isata and Sparrow out. It had been a long day. Sparrow and Isata sat on the porch before going into the house for the night. They sat in rockers next to one another and held hands; Sparrow was content, and Isata was just glad to have her baby back; she was looking forward to more nights like this.

Two days later, the Singleton family woke up bright and early to get ready for *Family & Friends Day* at Singleton's Kitchen. Everyone got dressed and ate a quick breakfast Isata prepared. Gentry dropped GirlChild off with Mama Maggie before he jumped in the truck with Isaac. Sparrow and Isata rode together. When they arrived at the restaurant, Duck had already opened.

Isaac's siblings, nieces, and nephews all gathered in the dining area. The restaurant would be closed for breakfast and would not open until lunch time. Isata and August counted heads until everyone was accounted for; they delegated tasks, and everyone went to their stations. Isaac and his brothers went into the kitchen to finish prepping food. The year prior, they had a turnout of about twelve hundred people.

This year, they expected more people due to August's promotional campaign. She had been on the news and in the newspaper. She passed out flyers at local shelters and soup kitchens. She even posted flyers at the airport and in museums for tourists to see. August wanted to make sure they reached as many people as possible.

Sparrow helped her cousins Isabella and June fold the restaurant's new brochures that Duck had picked up from the printing company the night prior. They wanted to make sure every to-go bag had a brochure with information about the history of the restaurant, the menu, contact information and hours. The bag would also include a coupon for future use to redeem a free appetizer. Ola, Lillie, and Esther started on wrapping plastic silverware in napkins to include in the bags. Duck and his cousins, Charles, Abraham, Jackson, and Sampson used their separate vehicles to transport chairs and tables back and forth from local churches to fill the parking lot.

Everyone was chipping in and playing their part. They worked for the next few hours until everything was in place. Isata sent Sparrow back over the bridge to pick up Mama Maggie and GirlChild. Isata phoned ahead to let Mama Maggie know Sparrow was on the way. Sparrow was excited about her first *Family & Friends Day.* She was proud of her family for always finding a way to serve the community and give back. She looked forward to participating in more family events.

Sparrow made it over the bridge to Mama Maggie's. She loaded the car seat into the back seat and strapped GirlChild in. Sparrow made sure to drive the speed limit with Mama Maggie and GirlChild in the car. Mama Maggie didn't go over the bridge often, so Sparrow wanted to make sure her grandmother was comfortable and felt safe. Mama Maggie turned down the radio.

"That smile looks good on you, Bird. What you smirking about?"

Sparrow kept her eyes on the road. "I'm just happy, Mama Maggie. This summer has arguably been one of the most stressful yet life changing summers ever."

"I can see that; you started off rough but you're finishing off smooth. I'm proud of you."

"Thank you. I think coming home has been one of my better decisions."

"We're lucky to have you back."

Sparrow pulled up to the back parking lot of the restaurant. She grabbed GirlChild's car seat with one arm and let Mama Maggie hold the other arm as she helped her grandmother out of the car. They entered the restaurant through the kitchen and were right on time. The lunch hour was going to kick off in ten minutes. Duck and the cousins had done a good job setting up the parking lot. There was a buffet set up in front of the restaurants wrap around porch and tables and chairs were set up in the parking lot. There were bounce houses for the kids and a snow cone truck. The media was also there.

Isata and Sparrow got Mama Maggie and GirlChild set up on the porch so Mama Maggie could see everything. Isaac and his brothers finished bringing food out to the buffet table and would replenish it as things ran out. Sparrow and her cousins got in place to serve. Reverend Hoyt walked up to the podium on the porch and tapped the mic. Once he had everyone's attention, he said a few words to acknowledge the Singleton family and their contribution to the community before saying grace. He passed the microphone to August, and she provided instructions to everyone on how to redeem their tickets for a plate.

For the next three hours, they served almost fifteen hundred people. They had a little food left over for some to get another serving. Mama Maggie watched from the porch with pride; her children and grandchildren were carrying on a legacy she never thought was possible. August spoke to the media and networked with community leaders; they discussed making next year's event even bigger and better. The cleanup committee from the church began to break down the buffet line to help relieve the Singletons. Sparrow went up onto the porch to check on Mama Maggie and GirlChild.

Mama Maggie was holding GirlChild in her lap. Sparrow made baby noises and faces until GirlChild cooed back. Mama Maggie's face turned sour when saw looked up and saw Amos Jennings walking up the stairs of the porch. "Sparrow, can we talk?" Sparrow turned around to the deep voice. *What the hell was he doing here?* She gave Mama Maggie a reassuring look. "I'll be back." She turned to follow Amos to the other side of the porch.

"What are you doing here?"

Amos tried to control his volume. "You burned me!"

"I burned you? I only did what you were going to do to my family, Amos. Do you think I'm stupid?"

"You had August tell my boss I tried to seduce you. Imagine how that looks!"

"Imagine trusting a man only to find out he's using you for his own selfish reasons. I'm sure there are other families you can go after, just stay away from mine."

Amos threw his hands up. "You know what, I didn't come here to argue."

"Well why did you come?"

"I came to say goodbye. Despite what you've done, I didn't want to just up and leave without seeing you."

"You could've saved yourself the trip."

Amos turned to leave but he turned back around to face Sparrow. "Just because I'm leaving doesn't mean this is over, they'll just send someone else to replace me."

Sparrow confidently fired back, "And we will be ready for them. That's the Singleton way."

www.ingramcontent.com/pod-product-compliance
Lightning Source LLC
LaVergne TN
LVHW090517110826
845146LV00003B/887

* 9 7 9 8 2 1 8 4 6 2 4 9 9 *